THE
BLOOD
CHRONICLES

THE BLOOD CHRONICLES

KIMBERLY LOVE

THE BLOOD CHRONICLES
THE HARLEY WOLFHART SERIES BOOK 2

Copyright © 2024 by Kimberly Love

All rights reserved.
Printed in the United States of America.

No part of this book may be used or reproduced in any manner whatsoever without written permission except in the case of brief quotations embodied in critical reviews or articles.

This book is a work of fiction. Names, characters, businesses, organizations, places, events and incidents either are the product of the author's imagination or are used fictitiously. Any resemblance to actual persons, living or dead, events, or locales is entirely coincidental.

Cover Design and Interior Design by We Got You Covered Book Design
WWW.WEGOTYOUCOVEREDBOOKDESIGN.COM

First Edition: March 2024

ONE

TODAY WAS THE DAY THAT *she was going to die.*

Harley Wolfhart was hunting the Butcher, or maybe he was hunting her, she really couldn't tell anymore.

She entered a room, and it was pitch dark. The shadows were deep as if the walls were painted black. She couldn't see anything. She almost expected to see red eyes piercing through the darkness.

"Dammit," she said. Not a good sign. Her Glock firearm raised; she walked slowly across the space. A scratch across the pavement had her spinning around only to have hands wrap around her throat. The pressure around her neck constricted tighter.

His eyes were glowing through the dark as she felt her breath escaping her. She struggled to no avail; he was so much stronger than she was. Blackness was coming to take her as Rayland smiled the same smile that was so familiar to her, a smile that she had believed she would never see again.

Harley couldn't breathe, her throat constricted and when

she opened her eyes, she saw him. His eyes cold, emotionless, not an ounce of life inside of them. Windows into a dark place, an evil place, where souls were eaten up. His hands were around her throat, squeezing tighter, she was choking but nothing was coming out. She couldn't breathe and she was starting to feel faint. A smile formed on his face as life was leaving her body. He had finally found her, and he was going to kill her.

Rayland.

She was slowly fading away.

Harley screamed as she tore out of sleep. She thrashed from her covers feeling like they were suffocating her. She screamed until she couldn't anymore, her throat raw and torn. She was gulping at air now. She turned and picked up the glass of water that she kept on the side table beside her bed. She gulped it down.

Rayland. He was back.

Her t-shirt was soaked in sweat, and her hand went to her chest, rubbing at the area. Her heart slammed in her chest, and she could still feel where Rayland's hands had been around her neck. She pulled off her t-shirt and dropped it on the floor. She laid back down and pulled the sheets around her naked body.

Was she going to die that day? That was still up for debate.

She remembered back to the call that she received in her office. She had been so excited, finally opening her own private investigator's firm, starting over from the horrors of the island. A call had come in; she had thought it had been one of her friends calling to congratulate her, but then that voice.

She would never forget that voice. She would never forget the horrors that she witnessed on the island. She had never fully recovered from the time. It had only been a few short months ago but it still felt like it was yesterday.

She had hung up on Rayland and immediately called her old friend Chief Aat from Thailand to find out what had happened. He wasn't there. Instead, Officer Ned told her a chilling tale about how the Chief had gone missing and they had found his dismembered remains in the tin mines just like the others had been found. It had started again. Her hands had shaken the entire time. Chief Aat was gone and at the hands of Rayland. No one could figure out how he had managed to escape. Thailand prisons often failed to meet international standards with inmates put in overcrowded cells, and often misplaced. Even Ted Bundy managed to escape from prison multiple times. Everyone thought that the killer was no longer a threat, and they couldn't have been more wrong. She remembered the room with the severed head and wondered if they ever found Chief Aat's head. She refused to ask.

After finding out that Rayland had escaped prison, Harley had every reason to wonder if she would survive another day. Rayland or better known as The Butcher was one of the most brutal killers she had come in contact with and now he was on the loose.

He also now knew where her office was and how to get a hold of her. Hell, he could even know where she lived. He had the advantage over her. He knew where she was, and she had no idea where he was. It was no wonder she was having nightmares now that a sadistic killer was hunting her. She knew that it was going to be up to her to go after him. What choice did she have? She wasn't going to wait around for him to come after her. She would have to find him and soon, but she wasn't foolish enough to say that the very thought didn't terrify her to the core.

She could only assume at that point that he was watching her. She crawled out of bed, quickly dressed, and went towards the kitchen in search of coffee.

She hopped up on the counter as the coffee percolated beside her. The smell alone could put her in a good mood. Her phone was charging on the counter, and she unplugged it and made a long-distance call to Thailand. Ned Ornlamai was an officer that had helped aid her in finding the vacation murders killer while she was there. They had become good friends.

"Ned here."

"How could you not tell me?"

"Harley?"

"You know damn well who it is."

"I'm so sorry our call yesterday was so abrupt. I left you with horrific news without really explaining anything. You should have been the first person I called when it happened. We've just been knee-deep in it."

"You didn't think I should get a call right away? I put that fucker away."

"Harley, he's in Singapore. I didn't think that you were an immediate threat. We expect to grab him before he tries to leave the island. We have men at all the exit points."

She sighed. "He's already gone. I think he's in New York."

"What do you mean?"

"He must have had a plan, ID stashed somewhere, probably cash too. This isn't the first time that he escaped prison. God, Ned, after what he did to Aat, he must have been planning this for a while, seething in his cell. I still can't get what happened to Aat out of my head. It's like he's trying to finish what he started. Of course, he's coming after me."

There was a silence on the other end that was infinite.

"There's no way."

"He called me, Ned."

"No. Oh my god."

"I don't know where he was calling from, but he called my office, so he knows where I am."

"Do you have protection? I'm sure that your former co-workers from the NYPD would have your back. You could have 24-hour surveillance."

"I don't need protection."

"Harley don't be ridiculous. I would take protection after what happened to Chief Aat. You think we're not all over here watching our backs? I'm not even sure that I don't have a target on my back. Don't you go after this monster on your own. Anyone that has the Butcher after them needs protection."

"I'm not hiding from him, Ned. I'm going to bring him down once and for all."

"Harley, are you insane? You stay away from him. You almost died."

"I don't think that I have a choice. He's coming for me. I just have to find a way to be one step ahead of him. I need to know what his plan is, what he wants."

"He's insane. I don't think that he knows what he wants. I'll contact the NYPD and notify them that he could be in the area. They can start looking for him. Please, Harley, watch your back."

"How the hell did this happen? How did he get to Aat?"

"Well, none of us expected this. When we heard that he escaped, the last thing that we expected was for him to go seek revenge on anyone. We thought he would try to get off the island as soon as possible. No one thought Aat was in danger. We thought he was going to be focused on getting off the island or going into hiding. Unfortunately, we were looking in the wrong direction."

"He should have been put in the hole or put to death."

"If I had a say in it, he would have been hung."

Harley would have laughed if her heart wasn't thundering in her chest.

"I need to get to the office, Ned. Keep me posted on

any developments."

"Will do. Stay safe, Harley."

She clicked off the call and set her phone down.

Where was Rayland? Was he planning on coming for her next or did he have another victim in mind? She shuddered at the thought of running into him again. She should have killed him instead of giving him the opportunity to get free again. But who could have predicted that? Sipping her coffee, she thought about what she was going to do next. How could she begin to look for a ghost?

Harley grabbed her car keys and left her home. The moment she got outside, a shiver went up her spine. The sounds of the world waking up were all around her, but she felt watched. She surveyed the streets and the windows in the homes around her, but she didn't see anything that concerned her. Did he know where she lived, or was she overreacting?

She made her way to her car while on high alert. Once inside, she took a look around again. Nothing. It was a short drive to her office, under five minutes and she kept looking in the rearview mirror to see if she was being followed.

Once in the office, she went to her desk. She sat down and opened her laptop.

Danny Kelly walked through the door briskly, multiple coffees in hand. The man with two first names.

"I thought that you could use this after the day that you had yesterday."

Harley smiled and took the coffee from him. Danny was new to the company. Danny was a private investigator that was there to help her share the caseload that she was quickly accumulating. After the media fire that happened once she had got off the island, she was pretty much fully booked a year in advance. She still got calls every day for her to look into cases, and she was at the point now where she was turning them down. Danny would be the first of many hires that would be happening in the next few weeks, but for now, she had bigger problems. She hadn't realized that going on talk shows to talk about the Butcher was going to make her so popular. She had also hired an assistant and receptionist, but Danny would essentially be her right-hand man.

He was a bulky 6'3", formidable man who towered over her. He had a small amount of scruff that he never seemed to shave off, but it suited him. He had kind, hazel eyes and a strong jawline.

"Thank you, Danny."

"How are you doing with the whole thing?"

She glanced down at the laptop as she said, "Oh, you mean the fact that I'm being stalked by a sadistic killer. Yeah, coffee will fix that."

He chuckled. "Roxie told me to give you these messages. They seem important."

He handed her papers, and she looked down at them.

"What the hell?"

"What is it?"

"I got a message from Rayland's mother. She wants to speak with me."

"You're kidding. Have you spoken to her before?"

"No. She was at the trial. I know that the Chief spoke with her after the arrest. But I had no interest in speaking to the person responsible for Rayland."

"And now? How are you going to handle this?"

She looked up from her laptop. "I think that now that Rayland is back, I should probably sit down with this woman and see if she has some answers for me."

He shrugged. "There must be a reason why she wants to talk to you."

"Exactly."

"What's the other one? Anything I can handle?"

Harley stared at the paper.

"It looks like someone wants me to evaluate a case they're working on. They're having trouble catching the killer. Why don't you make contact and see about getting me some more information. We can probably go see them together."

"Okay, will do."

He turned and left the office, and she leaned back in her chair. Rayland's mother. Harley couldn't remember the woman's name. The message was only signed with the woman's last name, Mrs. Armstrong. But for the life of her, she couldn't remember her first name. When she thought back to the vacation from hell, her whole body would grow cold.

She had gone to Thailand to find herself after her

partner Chris had died at her arms. The truth was, she had been the one to kill him. She had discovered too late that he was a dirty cop and she ended up having to pull a gun on him. It didn't end well.

She sought out Thailand to get some rest and healing, but it hadn't quite turned out that way. She did end up finding herself, but during that process, she had seen multiple friends die, a lover die, and she had almost lost her own life to a crazy psychopath. She still had nightmares from the things that she saw on the island. She also held a lot of guilt for not being able to save her friends from the horrific deaths they endured. She still had Keri, whom she met on the island, but not being able to save her sister was something Harley struggled with. Keri didn't hold her responsible for any of it which she was eternally grateful. The two were the only survivors of the island killings.

She had finally accepted that she was safe from the Butcher, but now he was back. She could only assume he meant to kill her that time. His ruthlessness was almost supernatural, and she was starting to wonder if he was like the monsters in the old slasher films she used to watch when she was a teenager. Could he be killed? He sure had a hard time being held behind bars.

She could still picture Rayland's smile. It was probably something she would never forget. It was the smile that had won her over in the first place. He was easily one of the handsomest men that she had ever come into contact with. How could she have been fooled by him? She beat herself up a lot about that. He was a master manipulator, and he had the ability to put a mask on and fool anyone that he hunted.

It didn't hurt that he was ridiculously charming and witty. It was hard for people to believe that someone who was attractive could be capable of heinous acts. But his looks made it easy for women to go off alone with him.

She fondled the paper and thought about what she could possibly say to Rayland's mom. What did she feel she needed to say to Harley?

She picked up the office phone and dialed the number on the paper. She listened to the ringing, and it was picked up on the third ring.

"Hello?"

"Mrs. Armstrong, it's Harley Wolfhart. You wanted to speak with me?"

"Call me Savannah."

"Okay, Savannah. How can I help you?"

"I'm sure you heard the disturbing news that Rayland is free."

I swallowed hard. "Yes, I have."

"You should have killed him."

"Excuse me?"

"You should have killed him, Harley. You should never have allowed that evil to have another chance to kill again. Now, he's going to come for me, and you as well, I suspect."

She wasn't wrong. There were times that she wished

she would have had the strength to kill Rayland. But she had barely survived her exchange with the Butcher. She could still feel his hands around her throat, squeezing the life out of her.

She sighed. "Savannah, is there a reason that you called me?"

"I would like to meet with you, Miss Wolfhart. My son seems to have a certain fascination with you. Maybe we can help each other stay alive."

Harley shuddered. "Please call me Harley."

"Will you come to New Orleans to meet with me?"

Harley hadn't expected to be doing any road trips right away with having just opened up her office.

"You might not be aware, but I just newly opened an office and now isn't the best time."

"Do you want to stay alive, or not?" Savannah snapped.

Uhhh, well sure, she thought to herself sarcastically. She didn't know what to say to the woman.

"Please, Harley."

Harley sighed. "Let me look at my schedule and get back to you, but I'm not making any promises."

"Thank you."

Harley hung up the phone. Danny came back into the room. She looked up. "What do you have for me?"

"The Cherokee County Georgia Sheriff's Department is requesting your presence with a case. It literally just happened. A woman showed up to a hospital with a gunshot wound. There were two kids in the backseat, all with gunshots. One dead, one critically injured. A ten-year-old little girl and an 8-year-old boy."

Harley raised a brow. "Really?"

"She said it was a carjacking. A man tried to get into the vehicle, shot up the whole thing and she managed to get away."

Harley's brow furrowed. "That seems highly unlikely. Unless she's incredibly lucky."

"She might be."

"Well, it seems pretty open and shut. What do they need me for?"

He smiled. "They are impressed with your famous story of taking down a serial killer."

She groaned. "I almost died."

"Nonetheless, you are a Queen in their eyes," he said laughing, "They would like you to come in and advise as an expert on the case. See if you can bring any new insight."

Harley pinched the bridge of her nose. "They think that she did it, don't they?"

"Yes."

"Her own kids. Can the other child make a statement?"

"Too soon to tell. They're not even sure that the kid will make it. She's in pretty rough shape."

"God, how do mothers become monsters?"

"There's a video."

She looked up at him. "Of what? Let's see it."

"They sent it to your email. It's her initial statement."

She opened her email and clicked on the link to

the video. A young woman popped up, sitting in an interrogation room. She wasn't much older than her early 30's. She had a blonde pixie cut and ice-blue eyes. She looked like the last person in the world that would ever kill someone. But she had learned a hard lesson that looks could be deceiving. That was how those monsters got away with their crimes. When a killer stood trial, it could be difficult to convict if they appeared to not be a monster. People didn't want to believe that the handsome man that lived next door might put them in a freezer.

Harley watched the testimony of the woman as she talked about the guy who attacked her and her children while they were parked at a camping site. She described the horrendous acts that were done to her children.

"How long after the incident was this interview conducted?"

"As soon as she was discharged from the hospital. She was shot in the arm, so no real danger. I think she was there for two days. They got her patched up and the sheriff's department brought her in for questioning the same day."

"And one kid is dead?"

"Yes, why, what are you thinking?"

"She's so calm, like a waveless ocean."

He looked at the screen again and nodded.

"Shouldn't she be hysterical or, at the very least, sad? A few tears would be nice. She's cold, even emotionless. Seriously, she's gone through a terrible experience and one of her children is dead. She might lose both of her children in the next 48 hours, but she's cool as a cucumber."

"It's like she's recalling her experience of going through the grocery store."

"Right. Makes no sense."

"So, what are you gonna do?"

She looked up at him. "Want to go on a road trip?"

He shrugged. "Sure, why not? Do you really think that she tried to kill them? Why?"

"Who knows why? It could be for a million reasons. Sometimes the most bizarre reasons make sense to them. Most often it's because they are just over being parents. It was too hard for them, ya know?"

She picked up the phone and dialed her assistant.

"Hey, Roxie. I need you to book a flight for Danny and me to go to Georgia. Set us up with a hotel and a car rental. We'll be heading to New Orleans next."

"New Orleans," he mouthed to her. She silenced him with a finger.

"Also, I need you to call Mrs. Armstrong and let her know I'll be stopping by tomorrow."

Danny's eyes widened.

She hung up the phone. "Alright, get your matters in order. We're likely going to be gone a week."

"What made you decide to go see Mrs. Armstrong?"

"Well, it's probably best that I get the hell out of New York for a bit. It's likely that Rayland has camped out here for the time being."

Roxie floated into the office and rattled off her itinerary.

"Great! Thank you. Roxie, I need you to go through the resumes and hire two more investigators."

"You want me to do the hiring?"

"Yes, I trust your judgement. There really isn't much choice. I don't know how long I'm going to be gone and we have a ton of cases piling up. I need someone to start working on these. Hire at least two and get them started with the most recent cases, and start clearing off the caseload."

"Will do." She left the room.

She looked at Danny. "Go home, we leave at ten."

He saluted her and left the office. She turned back to the cool, calm eyes that looked back at her from the monitor.

Harley wasn't a fan of flying. She preferred road trips but taking a twenty-hour drive wasn't realistic. They had a job to do, and they already had two stops to make. She felt a little cramped in her window seat as Danny was a large man. She should have opted for the aisle seat.

"Why did you decide to go to Louisiana if the Georgia Sheriff's Department is waiting for us?"

She looked over at him.

"Because I imagine the Sheriff's Department is fully

capable of handling this case without me. There is a dangerous serial killer on the loose which seems more important right now."

"Shouldn't you leave that to the FBI? They must be involved in the search by now."

"I'm sure that they are. And I would love nothing more than to not be involved in this, but Rayland hasn't left me much choice. I don't just want to sit around waiting for the day that he finds me. I want to do something."

"Maybe you should hire some protection."

"Ugh, what is with you, men? I don't want protection. I'm not helpless. Rayland could kill me in the next 24 hours if I don't find him first. Hiding in a room with a guard out front isn't going to help catch the Butcher. I have no idea how his mother thinks that she can help but I know he mentioned his mother to me before he was shot. There's something there, I just need to find it."

"He's that bad, is he?"

She nodded. "He's worse than you could ever imagine." She suddenly got lost in thought before she turned to him again. "You didn't see his trophy room. For the record, he tends to take out anyone associated with me. So, watch your back."

"I'm not worried," he said with a wink.

"Do not underestimate him, Danny. You'll regret it. It doesn't matter how big you are."

He nodded. She decided to change the subject.

"Are you married? Do you have any children?" *Anyone that would miss you if you died,* she thought silently.

"I have a girlfriend and no children. It's just starting to get serious. She just moved in."

"How does she feel about you going away for a week?"

"Well, she's gotten used to me traveling for work. Though, I don't have to do it that often. She was more concerned about the fact that my boss is hot. Her words, not mine. I don't think you're hot at all."

Harley smirked. "Tell her she has nothing to worry about. I'm far too emotionally damaged to get involved with anyone, least of all an employee. Besides the last time that I got involved with a partner, I ended up shooting him on the job."

"Alright, noted."

Harley put her headphones in and tuned into the movie playing. "Oh, Jerry McGuire, my favorite."

TWO

"CHRIS, IF YOU DON'T FIND us a coffee shop, I'm going to lose it."

We had reached New Orleans and were driving around a suburban area called Mandeville. It was one of those quiet neighbourhoods that people sought out because they believed it was safe to raise a family. Of course, that was where Rayland grew up, so safety was sometimes an illusion. Harley could never understand how people lived in a small town. *Where the hell was the Starbucks?* At that point, she would even settle for a Dunkins.

"How about Mama Tots Diner? I bet they have coffee."

Harley raised an eyebrow as they pulled in.

"Just don't expect a vanilla latte here."

She laughed. When they walked in, all heads turned towards them. It was the exact moment that you knew that they knew you were an outsider. They went up to the bar and Chris ordered a couple of coffees to go.

"What size?" The waitress asked.

He didn't even look at Harley when he said, "As large as you can make them."

They weren't far from Savannah's place, and she would need all the help that she could get to survive the meeting.

Coffee in hand, they left the diner and headed towards Savannah's home. When they pulled up, Harley was surprised to see that the house looked so normal. It was a two-story house with a white picket fence. There was a front porch with a swing. It was almost too wholesome. She wasn't sure what she expected. Maybe a dark, broken-down home, the kind that you expect to see in horror movies.

"This was his childhood home?"

Harley startled and looked at Danny. "Creepy, right? Yes, this is his childhood home. Crazy to think that a psycho could be made in a place like that."

"Made or born."

She shrugged. "Who knows? Alright, let's get this over with."

They exited the rented Lincoln SUV. They made their way to the front door and Harley knocked. After a few moments, Savannah answered with a big smile on her face.

"Oh, thank God, you're here."

Harley raised her eyebrows. "Is everything, okay?"

Savannah was the epitome of aging gracefully. She could probably still be a beauty queen. She had to be pushing 65 and yet her skin was flawless, and her shocking red hair looked like she just had a fresh blow-out and had returned from the spa.

"Yes, come in."

They followed her inside. Her home was warm and inviting with the smell of cinnamon in the air. Harley could picture Rayland growing up there, surrounded by warmth and love. Every piece of furniture in the home looked lived in, and there were family photos all over the walls. What had gone wrong with Rayland? They followed her into the living room and sat down on the couch. Savannah sat in a chair across from them. She had a glass of iced tea beside her.

Harley stared at the condensation on the glass waiting for Savannah to say something. Savannah just stared back at them, and Harley was starting to think that they were stuck in some parallel universe. She glanced at Danny who looked too large for the room. She smiled and turned back to Savannah.

"Savannah, have you heard from Rayland at all?"

"No. That's not the way our relationship works. We haven't spoken in 17 years, nor have I seen him, until the trial, of course. And still, I've never spoken to him."

"It was nice of you to be there to support him."

Savannah scoffed. "I was doing no such thing. The only reason why I was there was to make sure he was locked up for good. A lot of good that did."

A chill went up Harley's spine.

"Tell me, Harley, how did they manage to let that monster slip through their fingers?"

"I wish I knew. I'm so sorry, Savannah. I wish I could have stopped him. He almost killed me. I think they should have extradited him to the United States instead of leaving him in Singapore. It's too late for that now."

She waved Harley's comment away. She couldn't help but feel responsible for everything. She should have stopped him. Now he was loose and doing God knew what.

"Can you tell me about his childhood?"

Savannah shuddered. "He was never a normal boy. I could see that right away. He wasn't the kind of child that ran into your arms for hugs and kisses. I thought it was a little weird, but the doctors always told me that it wasn't anything to be worried about. Some kids are just shy and aloof. He was a boy and not all boys were huggers. That's what they told me. I didn't understand him. He always used to look at me strangely, like he was trying to figure me out."

"What do you mean?"

"I would catch him staring at me. But it wasn't like how you catch someone else staring. He would have this glazed look on his face like he really wasn't there. He was somewhere else while he was looking at me. It was very disconcerting."

Harley knew exactly the look she was talking about. It was unnerving, to say the least.

"The one difference between him and a lot of killers that you read about was that he wasn't some loner. They always say that in those shows on TV. 'He never had any friends. He was bullied. Girls didn't like him.' My boy was popular. I'm sure it had a lot to do with the fact that he grew up to be quite the handsome young man. He certainly had weird tendencies, but he kept them close. I was really the only one that saw who he really was and that's because he wanted me to."

"Why do you think that is?"

She took a drink from her glass and appeared lost in thought.

"Savannah."

"He sensed my discomfort with him early on. I had seen some things. When he was younger, I saw things I wished I had never seen. I didn't know how to deal with it. To be honest, I feared my own son, and he knew it. I was young, his father had left, and I just couldn't deal with it."

Harley waited, feeling like she still had more to say. Sometimes it was best to wait someone out before talking.

"I think he wanted me to love him no matter what, and I couldn't. That might sound monstrous from a mother, but I knew he was evil, maybe not even human. I saw him, I mean really saw him and I was probably the only one that did. I saw right inside him, and he wanted me to still love him at his darkest. He resented me when I couldn't. Not that I ever told him that, but kids know when something's missing. He knew that I was disgusted by him."

Chris spoke up. "What kinds of things did you see, ma'am."

Savannah sighed. "One day he had been gone from the house for awhile. His bike was still in the front yard, so I knew he must be close by. He was probably close to 11 at the time. I found him in the shed in the backyard. I rarely used it, it used to be his father's shop, so I never had any reason to be in there." She stopped as if she was collecting herself. "He was carving up some animal. I couldn't even tell what it was after what he had done to it." Tears were streaming down her face, as she recounted the horrors from her past.

"You have to understand, we didn't know about serial killers back then. I had no idea what he was really capable of. I just thought he might be unwell. I didn't know what to do."

"Does your son have a history of killing or torturing animals?"

"Yes. A lot of the neighbor's pets often went missing. I'm sure that's what was on the table that day."

"You didn't do anything about the fact that your son was killing the neighborhood pets?" Danny said, aghast.

"What could I do? Call the police on my own son? Who would do that?"

"Institutionalize him," Harley said softly. "At the very least. You know that he needed help."

Savannah was sobbing now. "How could I do that? If it was your child, you would do whatever you could to protect them. I could never have imagined what he was capable of until it was too late. My God, he was only 11. I thought maybe it was just the animals, maybe he just wasn't a fan of animals. I could never have imagined what happened on that island. Did you think that I didn't care? I always wondered if he was going to show up back here."

"What do you mean too late?" He asked.

"There was this girl, a teenager. I think they were dating, though he never really admitted to it. She was from his high school."

Savannah looked at Harley with dread.

"Go on."

"She went missing."

"Oh, God," Danny whispered.

"She was never found. No body. Nothing. Her poor parents."

"Rayland killed her."

Savannah nodded slowly. She wiped at her nose with a Kleenex. "I have no evidence, of course."

"Then, how do you know it was him?"

A smirk came across Savannah's face. "You knew him well, didn't you, Detective."

"I'm no longer on the force."

Savannah nodded. "It was him. I could see it written all over his face when I asked him about her. We never talked about it, but I knew."

Harley looked at Danny, whose face was reddening. She made eye contact with him and shook her head slowly. There was no point in getting heated.

"What happened to you thinking he just didn't like animals? Are you out of your mind? The lives you could have saved." His voice was ice cold.

Savannah looked at him. Her nose went in the air. "You don't understand."

"Did you see the pictures of those kids on the island? What he did to them. That's just the tip. He said he's killed 100's of people. You were at his trial; you saw what he did. If you would have talked to the police, had him institutionalized, all those people might still be alive."

She glanced at him. "He was my son."

"He was a monster. Barely human. He was no one's son. Maybe you should be held responsible for enabling a killer."

"I did no such thing."

Harley put her hand up to silence Danny. "Let's not get off track here. Savannah, you said before that you asked him to leave."

"Yes, it was after the girl went missing. I started worrying that he might kill me next."

Danny scoffed. Harley side-eyed him.

"I told him that I knew what he did. I told him that I would not stand for that type of behavior. I sent him away and told him to never return."

Harley ignored the glare that Danny was giving

Savannah. "That must have pissed him off. I imagine that didn't go over very well."

She cringed. "It was the most scared I've ever been. I wasn't sure how he was going to react. Or if he was going to hurt me."

"What did he do?"

"He came really close to me, our faces just inches away from each other. He was sneering at me." Savannah took a moment and picked up her glass of sweet tea. Her hands shook as she brought it to her lips. She took a sip, composing herself.

"A loving mother wouldn't send her son away," she whispered, "That's what he said to me. I told him that he was no longer my son and that I never wanted to see him again."

Harley tried to imagine what it would be like for Rayland to hear that his mother wanted nothing to do with him anymore. For any mother to say that to a child, she was completely warranted in her opinion, but it would still be hard for any child to hear from their mother. At 17 years old, Rayland's brain wouldn't have been completely formed at the time, and anything within his childhood could have impacted his future. Of course, he was already a serial killer by then. In Rayland's undeveloped and diseased mind, he would not have been able to see why his mother wasn't imparting unconditional love just like mothers are supposed to. Harley didn't have children of her own, but she couldn't imagine what it would be like to discover your child was a monster and not be able to do anything about it. Did she make the right decision? Probably not. She probably should have turned him in. But as a woman, Harley couldn't hate her for it; she completely understood how hard it must have been to say goodbye to her son and to continue to protect him at all costs. She knew if it was her, she wasn't sure she would have been able to turn her own son in either. It's easy to say you'll do the right thing until you're in the situation. It was Savannah's only child, and she probably wondered her whole life where she had gone wrong.

Harley remembered the things that Rayland said about his mother when they were in the abandoned hotel. The bitterness that dripped from his words. She wondered if Savannah knew.

"He kills women who look just like you."

It was like a bolt of lightning hit Savannah and even Danny looked stricken. "What are you talking about?"

"Did you really not compare the victims when you were there at the trial? The ones that he picked, were all redheads. I'm a redhead."

"No," she was shaking her head vehemently. "They weren't all redheads."

"No, some were even men. But those he picked to get them out of the way or to punish me. But all his victims, the chosen ones have all resembled you. He wants you dead, Savannah, he always has. That's why I'm here. Maybe there's a part of him that can't actually do it, but he wants to."

She stared stonily at Harley, the words making their desired impact. "I honestly thought he would pop up again. But he didn't. I never saw him again, until the trial. Not that he wasn't around."

"What do you mean?"

"I think he comes back from time to time, to check up on me. Sometimes I feel like someone is watching me; do you ever feel like that, Harley?"

A chill went up my spine. "Yes, I have."

"I suspect you have."

"Savannah, can I ask you a personal question?"

She shrugged.

"Why didn't you ever remarry? I mean, you must have had hundreds of suitors. You're a very beautiful woman. After all these years, you could still be a Beauty Queen."

Savannah brushed away a strand of hair, self-assured. There was no false modesty, she knew the power that she had over men.

"I've had many opportunities to get married again. I've been proposed to a lot."

Harley tried to hide her smile.

"I did date a few times and fell in love once with a wonderful man. He wanted to take care of me," Savannah said, her eyes glazing over as she got lost in a memory. "I thought that he might be the one. But Rayland grew terribly jealous, and accidents started happening around the house."

"What kinds of accidents," Danny asked.

"The kind that led to death. I caught Rayland setting one up and he passed it off as a prank. 'I'm just joking around, Mother.' I used to hate when he called me that. Made me feel like I was a hundred. I'm convinced he did it on purpose."

"You were worried that something was going to happen to the man you loved?"

She nodded, looking sadder than Harley had seen her.

"I broke things off with him. I didn't want to be responsible for something happening to him. To be honest, I think he was a little scared of Rayland himself. Rayland certainly had a way about him that would creep out the most hardened person. I broke it off with Johnson and he was sad for about five minutes, but I don't think that he could have packed fast enough."

"I'm sorry, that must have been hard."

"He wrote me years ago telling me how sorry he was. How much he regretted leaving me. It was hard to read but I knew that I did the right thing. I would never forgive myself if Rayland would have done something to him."

"But even after Rayland was gone, you didn't try again? Why? It must have been very lonely."

"I'm happy. Really, I am. I have my friends and my hobbies. I have thought about it. But look how he has invaded your life, never giving up on what he wants. I'm worried that if I fell in love again, that it would be the one thing that brought him back. I just never wanted to see him again. I never wanted to look in those eyes again. I've regretted going to that trial because I couldn't avoid his eyes."

The room grew still until Harley broke the silence.

"Rayland's high school girlfriend? That's just some cold case now? The parents really have no idea what happened to her?" His voice dripped with disgust.

"It's remained unsolved."

"How have you even remained living here? For all you know, that girl could be buried in your backyard."

Savannah shot up from her chair so fast that she knocked her side table, the tea spilling to the floor. "I want you out of this house right now. How dare you?"

Danny smiled while shaking his head. "You outta be ashamed of yourself."

"Danny, that's not helping. I'll meet you outside."

Danny stared at Savannah for a beat before turning and leaving the room. Harley waited until she heard the front door slam before turning back to Savannah. The woman had completely ignored the spilled drink. She was breathing hard.

"I'm sorry if he upset you."

Savannah didn't respond.

"Savannah, I'm going to speak with the sheriff in the area and have someone check in on you. They can have someone sit outside your home to make sure Rayland doesn't come here."

She was calming down now. "Yes, I think that would be a good idea."

"We are staying at the Comfort Inn in the area until

tomorrow, please contact me if you have any further information or if you hear from Rayland."

"Are you sure that you can't say longer, just in case?"

"No, I can't. We have to be in Georgia."

"I'm sorry that I can't be of more help."

"You did just fine, Savannah, we need to know as much as we can about Rayland. Get in his head so to speak to anticipate his next move."

"I'm surprised he kept you alive."

Harley blinked. "I don't think he meant to."

"Yes, he most certainly did."

Harley wasn't sure what she meant, but she did know that she wanted to get out of the house. The air in the room had become stifling.

Harley got up from the couch.

"I'll be in touch."

Savannah slowly sat back down in the chair, the spilled tea continuing to be ignored. She wasn't going to walk her out and Harley was fine with that. She made her way to the door, opened it, and quickly exited the house. Danny was standing on the porch. Harley sped-walked to the car.

"What is your hurry?"

"It's time to leave."

"No shit, but I'm not much of a fan of jogging."

"Why don't you look up a place to eat," Harley said as she got behind the wheel. She sat there and stared at the house. It no longer looked warm and inviting.

"That was weird at the end, right?" Danny said.

"Yes," She whispered. "Yes, it was."

"How do you know that she's not setting a trap for you?"

Harley's head snapped towards him. "You can't be serious? She's not helping him."

"You could have fooled me. She should have had that boy locked up a long time ago."

"Speaking of which, agitating her probably isn't the best way to get her to be forthcoming."

"She invited us here and she pissed me off. There are parents out there that have no idea what happened to their daughter."

"Right, but she doesn't have to talk to us. I would like to get some information out of her, and you were just aggravating her."

"I don't care, Harley. As far as I'm concerned, she's just as monstrous as her son. I don't even think that we got anything valuable from her."

"You don't?"

"Aside from the fact that he's obsessed with you, and you bear a striking resemblance to his mother. Yes, it was a fresh insight to discover that he's in love with his own mother. Being with you was probably like fucking his mother."

Harley closed her eyes and groaned.

"Too far?"

"Yes, geez. What am I supposed to do with that information? You think he was with me because of his mother? Gross."

"Not that you don't have a lot of good qualities."

She turned to him. "Danny, will you please shut the fuck up for five minutes? Find us somewhere to eat, please. I'd like to try to forget all the mental images you just put into my head."

She turned the ignition key and the SUV rumbled to life. She slowly backed out of the driveway and hoped that she would never have to see that place again.

THREE

HEADING TO GEORGIA, HARLEY HAD a lot of time to think. She was tempted to cancel her appointment with the Cherokee County, Georgia Sheriff's Department because she still wasn't sure why she was invited. When Rayland had been brought down, there was a lot of media attention on her. She had non-stop requests for media interviews. Everyone wanted to know how she had not only survived the notorious serial killer but how she had brought him down. He had almost killed her, so she didn't really think of herself as some kind of hero. But the world wanted to know who she was. She was offered a promotion to Detective with the NYPD, but she turned it down because she wasn't sure she wanted to work in a world with so much evil. She also wasn't sure who she could trust. Before she had even gone to Thailand, she was unsure that she ever wanted to be a cop again. Finding out your best friend and partner was a dirty cop was enough to make you wonder if you could trust anyone. Dirty cops were everywhere, unfortunately, and it went against everything she believed in as a cop. She loved her work, but she decided that being part of the police force just wasn't the same after Chris died.

Now, Rayland was back, and she had no idea where he was. She wasn't sure how she was going to get through another round with Rayland but if she got the chance, she would kill him the next time.

She felt bad for Savannah, knowing how much of her life she gave up because she was scared of her own son. She had lost the love of her life and had turned her back on her son. She was always afraid he would come back so she had spent her life alone, scared that her son would keep taking things from her. It was tragic thinking about it. She knew what it was like to lose someone and to spend a lot of time alone because of it. Was that going to be Harley's fate too?

So many tragedies were wrapped up in one person's life. The domino effect of having known Rayland was immense. How many people died because Savannah didn't say anything? The thought of it took her breath away. Danny had made it impossible for her to stop thinking about Rayland's high school girlfriend and what had really happened to her. When did Rayland start removing the heads from his bodies? If they knew enough of his victims, they would know when that fixation started. Or maybe it was always there. Was that the fate of the young girl as well? She shuddered.

The family needed closure and Harley intended on giving them that.

After they left Savannah's home, they stopped at a Texas Roadhouse and drowned their sorrows in steak and beer. They had returned to their separate hotel rooms to get some rest before hitting the road the next day.

She wasn't sure how she was going to handle the next interview, but she was fine with taking her time before returning home. She wasn't sure if Rayland was still in New York, but she was content with being as far away from him as possible. Traveling around for the time being made her feel just a little safer. She needed to devise a plan to deal with Rayland before he surprised her. She had considered setting a trap, but she had no idea which way he was going to be coming. He was holding all the cards, and he hadn't revealed anything to her that might give her some idea of what his next steps were. She was at his complete mercy and that wasn't a great place to be in.

Pulling up to the Sheriff's Department, Harley took a moment to collect herself.

"They should have called me by now, to cancel."

"I think you're putting way too much faith into this Mother."

Harley groaned. "I think I've had enough of mothers who fail their children. She couldn't possibly have tried to shoot her children. It's repulsive."

Danny didn't look convinced, and it made her feel

a little ill.

"Okay, let's get this over with before I change my mind."

They got out of the SUV and made their way inside the building. She approached the reception desk where a large deputy was doing paperwork. He had skin the color of dark chocolate and didn't smile when she approached. He barked out what she could only guess was a greeting.

"I'm looking for Sheriff Bradley Judd. I'm Harley Wolfhart, and he's expecting me."

He grunted at her and instantly disliked him. "Can I get your name?"

"Deputy Winn."

She stared at him until he turned and disappeared down a hallway. Harley turned to Danny who had a grin on his face. "Man, what a dick!"

She smiled. "I hope we'll see him as little as possible. Could you imagine who must have to sleep with that?"

"Maybe he's not getting any action at home."

Harley laughed.

The Deputy returned and Sheriff Judd was following behind him. The Sheriff grinned as soon as he saw her. Now that was the reaction she expected from the Deputy.

"Miss Wolfhart, we have been anticipating your arrival. Ya'll have no idea the chaos that's been going on here."

Harley smiled. "I appreciate the invite, I'm not sure

how I can help, but I will do what I can."

"Ma'am, there's no need to be modest. I've read everything written about you. You went up against one of the worst human beings on the planet and lived to talk about it. You're exactly who I want to talk to."

She felt her face burn. She refused to look at Danny.

"Sheriff, I would like to introduce you to Danny Kelly. He works for me at my office. He's one of my investigators."

"Welcome Danny. The more the merrier." They shook hands and then the Sheriff motioned for them to follow him.

"Come with me."

Harley and Danny both walked behind the reception desk and followed the Sheriff down the hallway. She wasn't sure what to expect or who she was going to meet. They followed him into a room with a window that showed into an interrogation room. There was a couple of detectives in the room sitting across from a woman. Harley recognized her from the video that the department sent her. She was stoned face, but she appeared to be cooperative.

"Sheriff, why hasn't she been released? There must be more going on than I was told."

"She actually is free to go while we continue to investigate, but in just the day that she has been out of the hospital, she's already done a few media interviews. She does every interview requested of her."

"What?"

"Yeah, something wasn't adding up to us after she came in to speak to us and it got worse after she was released. There were reporters outside of the hospital and the interviews are creepy. She's not upset, not once has she shed a tear as she talks about her child being dead. Sometimes she even laughs during the interview. Who would be laughing at a time like this?"

"What about the eldest child?"

"She's still on the critical list. We're hoping that she's going to pull through so she can add some clarity to the situation."

"Does she know?"

"Not yet, she thinks they are all dead. She hurried out of the hospital too fast to tell her that she still had a child to worry about."

"Do you mind if I watch while you guys do the interview?"

"Actually, I was hoping that you would join me."

She raised an eyebrow. She sighed. "Alright, let's do this."

The sheriff knocked on the door. The two detectives got up from the table and came to the door. Harley watched the suspect who had a slight smile on her face. The detectives came into the room and the sheriff introduced them to her.

"She did it. She did it for sure. No one is that cool. Nice to meet you, Harley. We're glad you're here."

"This is one of my guys, Danny Kelly. He's assisting me on the cases we have."

The two detectives shook his hand. Harley turned back to the guys.

"What exactly do you have on her?"

"Not enough to hold her. Unfortunately, we have yet to recover the murder weapon. There was nothing at the scene of the crime. Aside from her eldest daughter, everyone else that was in the car is dead. We could take it to trial, but it would be a shit show. She could end up walking. We need more. We need her child to pull through, then we will know what really happened."

Harley looked through the window again, watching her. Female serial killers were rare. You just didn't see a lot of them. Out of all the serial killers, only twenty percent of them were women. It could be argued that women were just better at it and didn't get caught but it could also be said that women just don't kill. Except in the case of mothers. Mothers that killed their children were on the rise. It was something that she found inconceivable and yet, it happened more often than people assumed. Sometimes, it had to do with undiagnosed postpartum depression. Other times, the woman was just plain evil. Harley was going with the latter in that case. "Alright, hang tight, guys; I'm going to take Harley in."

"Do you mind if I take the file?" Harley asked the detective in front of her. He had a closed cropped military cut, with a sweet smile. His eyes were hazel and piercing. "Yeah absolutely, good luck in there."

Harley looked over at Danny. He smiled. "I'll be

here if you need me."

She smirked and then followed the sheriff into the interrogation room where the smile dropped from her face. As soon as she entered the room, she could feel the woman's eyes on her. There was zero curiosity in them, she was analyzing her, sizing her up.

"Is this the FBI?"

Harley's eyebrow raised. "Why would the FBI be here?"

She narrowed her gaze at Harley. "Shouldn't you be out looking for the man that did this? How many detectives need to be in here interviewing me?"

"I assure you, ma'am, we are doing just that. But we don't have a lot of details to go on," Sheriff Judd stated.

"I've told you everything that I can remember."

They sat down at the table, the sheriff across from her while Harley sat at the end of the table. She was determined to just observe. However, the sheriff had something else in mind. He turned to look at Harley. She sighed.

"Rebecca, can you please give me a rundown on what happened to you and your children from the moment you got into the car that day?"

Rebecca stared at Harley. "I've already told this to the officers multiple times. I feel that no one is even listening to me. You should be out there looking for the monster who killed my children. He's going to kill more people."

Where were her tears? Where was the passion that

should be an inflection in her voice. There was nothing there but fake outrage.

"As the sheriff has already told you, they are looking. There are a lot more detectives that work here than there are in this room. Settle in so we can have this conversation. The sooner we have all the details, the better chance we have of catching the killer."

She blinked. "Fuck you."

Harley smiled but stayed silent. She had all day to wait Rebecca out.

"Am I a suspect here?"

"Miss. Mayers, we are conducting an investigation. We have questions to ask you and it would help a lot if you would just give Harley a rundown again of what happened. It's important. After all, you do want the killer caught, don't you?"

She sighed lengthy and Harley rolled her eyes. It must be exhausting having to answer questions about the death of your child.

"I thought it would be great to take my kids to the park. It's more like a camping ground, there's a lake, whatever. We've been there lots of times so I didn't think that there would be any danger. No reason to think that we would encounter anything bad. My kids love it there."

She paused for effect. Harley almost laughed.

"We were there for a few hours, and we were packing up to leave. The kids were already in the car. I was still packing up outside when a man approached."

"What did he look like?"

She paused again, thinking. "He was tall, much taller than me. Brown hair, blue eyes."

A very basic description. "Did he have any distinguishing marks? Scars? Tattoos that you can remember?"

Her eyes widened. "Yes, yes, he did have a tattoo."

Harley looked at Sheriff Judd and he looked surprised. She hadn't mentioned a tattoo before.

"Where was the tattoo and what was it?"

"An… eagle on his arm."

"Which arm?"

"I don't remember."

"Try."

She squinted her eyes. "Umm…his right."

Harley nodded. "What happened next?"

"He said he wanted my car. I tried to pull the kids out, but he told me to just go. Leave them there and I couldn't. Who could? He didn't like that, so he just started shooting."

Harley looked at her incredulously. "He opened fire? He could have just thrown you out of the vehicle and left. He could have told the kids to get up and leave."

Rebecca swallowed hard. "Right?! I know that. I don't know why he did it. Do you really expect me to know why he did it? He was probably just one of those psychopaths you see on the news all the time."

"So did he shoot you first?"

"No. He shot the kids in the backseat. Both of them

were lined up back there. Sitting so precious and he killed them all. Then he turned and shot me."

"Did you try to stop him from shooting the children?"

Stunned, Rebecca said. "Of course, I did, of course I would, tha—that's how I got shot."

"You told us before that he turned on you and shot you outside of the car."

"My memory hasn't been right since the incident. You have no idea what it was like. Everything happened so fast."

"So how did you get out of this mess? He was the only one with a weapon."

"He ran away."

"He ran away," Harley repeated.

"Yes, I think he got scared off, maybe it finally hit him what he did and how much trouble he would be in. What could I do? I was on the ground at that point, and I just crawled back to the car and got inside. I looked in the backseat and everyone was dead."

"Did you check their pulses?"

"No. I could tell they were dead. I needed to get to the hospital."

"So, this man goes on a shooting spree, and still doesn't get the car? He just decides it's better to murder three people and then run away?"

Rebecca glared at Harley. "I've just been through hell. You don't know what it was like. I remember driving to the hospital and looking in the rearview mirror and Cindy was reaching out for me, blood pouring from her mouth."

Harley stared at her. That was the moment that the woman should have been sobbing. She couldn't imagine a mother seeing something like that knowing your children were dead or dying. Harley didn't say anything for a moment and then said, "We were notified recently that your eldest daughter Cindy survived the attack and is currently in a coma."

The sheriff blanched. He hadn't expected Harley to let the cat out of the bag.

Rebecca's face drained of all color. Bingo. Harley watched her mouth try to form words. She had no idea.

"You're lying."

"Why would I lie about something like that? It's good news, right? One of your children miraculously survived this terrible ordeal."

"Why didn't anyone tell me? All this time I thought that she was dead. How could you keep this from me?"

"We thought you knew. You were at the hospital. Didn't you inquire about your children? You didn't ask the nurses if your children survived?"

"But I thought they were dead."

The silence in the room was deafening.

"I want a lawyer."

"I figured as much."

They got up from the table. The moment she asked for a lawyer, the interview was over. They walked out of the interrogation room where the detectives were waiting.

"Let her go. She's lawyering up," the sheriff said and then turned to Harley. "What do you think?"

She looked through the two-way glass and then to Danny who nodded. "She did it. She's emotionally flat. Even when she found out her daughter was still alive, she only expressed outrage, not relief, no real emotion or love for the child left alive. She should have been relieved and happy, but she had no emotion other than anger. I suggest you make sure there's a deputy at the door of the kid's hospital room or she might go and try to finish the job."

One of the detectives left the room immediately.

"She is chilling," Danny said. "A cold monster. I wonder how long she's been planning to kill her own children. That story about her child reaching out. She already said that she thought they were all dead. If that story is true, that kid knew her mother tried to kill her and was reaching out for help."

"I'll never understand how a mother could do something so depraved," Harley added.

"You didn't see the car," the sheriff said in barely a whisper.

She turned to him and waited.

"She pulled up to the hospital. She was squalling but still no tears, no emotion, just screaming. The hospital staff removed the children from the car and the backseat was soaked in blood. She actually had the nerve to ask me if her car was ruined during interrogation. Who would be worried about their car right now? I've never seen anything like it. Those poor kids."

"Don't let her get away with it, Sheriff."

She nodded to Danny, and the three of them left the room, and they walked with him to his office.

"I appreciate you coming all this way, Harley. I know it was a hike for you."

"We were in the general area. I'm not sure how much I helped, but I would certainly like to be around to see her taken down. We're probably going to get a hotel. Stay a few days and see how this pans out."

"We need to trap her."

"I guarantee that woman didn't think this through when she did it. She's already falling all over her storyline. She thinks she can just blame it on someone else and get away with it," Danny said. "The problem is, she's a beautiful woman with an innocent face, and without concrete evidence, the jury is going to take one look at her and say there's no way she could kill her three children."

Harley nodded.

"You're right about that, son, which is why we wanted Harley to come in. You read people well. I've talked to your superiors; they hold you in high esteem. They were hoping you were going to stay with the force."

Harley decided to dodge that comment. "She's going to try to finish the job, I guarantee. She'll trip herself up. These people cannot stop thinking about their victims. If that kid witnessed something, she's not going to let her live to tell about it."

"We might have less of a chance trapping her now that she has a lawyer."

"This woman is a narcissist; she's not going to be able to help herself."

"I'm not sure if you heard but the Butcher escaped Singapore prison."

"What? No shit. How did that happen?"

She smiled. "Yeah, I don't know but I suddenly have my hands full."

"You're involved in the case?"

"No, I actually would prefer to have nothing to do with it. But he called me."

Sheriff Judd's eyes widened. "He's here."

"I can't confirm it, but I would be willing to bet money on it. It's horrific, so really, I don't have a choice. If I don't do something about it, I'm going to end up finding him at the end of my bed one night."

The sheriff laughed. "I'm sorry, it's really not funny."

"It's okay, it's better to laugh than to start screaming."

"I would not want to be in your shoes, but if you need anything and I mean anything, you let me know. At this point, this is going to turn into a nationwide hunt if he's in the United States."

"Well, I pray he comes nowhere near you guys. What about the children's father? Has he been looked into at all?"

"Yeah, he had nothing to do with this. He's some deadbeat that rarely sees the kids."

One of the detectives swung his head into the office. "Sheriff, you're going to want to see this. She's on the news."

"Who? Rebecca? You have to be pulling my leg."

They all followed the detectives out of the office to a room with TVs. The local news was on, and Harley saw Rebecca standing outside the entrance to the hospital.

"Oh, my god, she's doing an interview."

It was like watching a trainwreck and none of them could look away. Rebecca was doing an interview outside of the hospital and even though she was talking about her dead children, she was ice cold. Not a shred of emotion. The only time she got even remotely heated up was when she talked about the interview with Harley and the sheriff.

"They think it was me. They think that I could hurt my own babies. My daughter is still alive, and they won't let me see her. She's in there and there's an officer outside her door who won't let me see her. She needs me. My lawyer said he could get me in there, but there would always be an officer present. They're treating me like a criminal."

The interviewer said, "You are very lucky to be alive."

"Oh, I'm not lucky. I can barely bend over to tie my shoes because of my arm. My daughter Cindy is lucky." Rebecca said with a laugh. "You don't know what I've been through." "It's just I, I, I...all she thinks about is herself," Harley said.

"Yeah, but she's laughing in the interview," Chris muttered.

"Her lawyer is going to lose it. She should not be doing interviews, especially since she's incapable of shedding a tear for her dead children," the Sheriff added.

"There's a guy out there. A really bad guy and the cops aren't even looking for him. I doubt this is the first time he's done something like this. How hard is it to look for a blonde-haired man? But they won't because they're accusing me of hurting my kids. What kind of mother could I be?"

Harley frowned. "Didn't she say the guy had brown hair during our interview?"

The sheriff smiled. "She sure did. Hell, maybe we should just let her keep doing interviews. She'll bury herself."

"Her lawyer is going to make a request for her to see her kid."

"Trust me, I will be doing everything in my power to make sure that doesn't happen. Even if she gets in that room, she'll never be alone with that child. I'll stand at the foot of her bed if I have to."

Harley's phone started ringing. She pulled it out of her pocket and looked at it. She didn't recognize the number. She clicked on the call and said hello.

"Darling, where have you been?"

A chill went up her spine. "Rayland, what do you want?"

Both Danny and the Sheriff turned around, eyes wide.

"Talking with Mother is playing dirty. You won't find anything out through her, she's a manipulating bitch, who lies."

He knew she had seen his mother. Was he following her? Was he in Georgia now? He was like a ghost, and she was going to lose. He knew where she was, and she had no idea where he was.

"Where are you? You know this isn't going to end well for you, Rayland. Turn yourself in, otherwise I'm putting you in a box in the ground."

He chuckled. "That fire inside of you, Harley, that's what I loved most about you. The things that we could do together."

"Fuck you."

"Now that's not nice. Who is the guy, Harley? Not another lover, I hope."

Harley glanced at Danny, and they made eye contact.

"He works for me, that's all."

"Hmmm, I don't like it."

"I don't care."

"He might."

"Rayland, stop. You're not going to get away with this. Stop while you still have a chance."

"How did the interview go?"

"Interview?"

"With the baby killer. She's just like me. There's something beautiful about a woman that can kill. You should give it a try sometime."

Harley froze. Rayland was in town. She knew that

now. Maybe he had been following her since New York.

"What do you mean, she's just like you?"

"She's done this before."

"You think she's killed before? Why do you say that?"

"You can see it in her eyes. Can't you see it by now, Harley? Can't you see what's in people's eyes?"

She knew one thing for sure, if she allowed him to keep talking, she was going to start screaming.

"Look at her past. She's killed before."

He was helping her. Why?

"Are you scared of me, Harley?"

A little bit. She swallowed hard. "No."

"I don't believe you. Maybe it's time that I make you scared of me again."

"You can't possibly think that you're getting away with any of this."

"I need to start cleaning up some loose ends."

"What does that mean? What are you going to do?"

"I have some things in my past that need to be dealt with."

"Rayland---"

The call clicked off and she was listening to a dial tone. What did he mean by that? Her phone rang again, and she jumped.

"What the hell is going on, Harley?" Danny asked.

She stared down at her phone, afraid to answer it. She clicked on the call. "Rayland?"

"Good god, has he found you too?"

Harley blinked. Not recognizing the voice. "Who is

this?"

"Heavens. It's Savannah. We just spoke a few days ago."

"I'm sorry Savannah, I just spoke with your son, and I'm a little rattled."

"So, he has found you too?"

"What do you mean? Has he called you?"

"No, I saw him here. He was outside my home. He's here, and I think he's going to kill me."

He said that he needed to clean up some loose ends from his past, she thought. Is that what he meant? Was he going to go back to where it all started and kill his mother?

"Are the officers still outside of your home?"

"Yes, but they said they didn't see anything. I know he was there."

"Let me make some calls and see who oversees the investigation now. If he's officially in the United States now, it's out of Singapore jurisdiction."

Harley clicked off the call. Danny looked at her questioning. "I think Rayland is going to kill his mother. We might have to make a trip back to Louisiana."

She scrolled through her contacts until she found her former Captain's phone number. She clicked on it and listened to it ringing.

"Harley, God, I'm thrilled you called."

"Hey Captain, I'm sure you're aware of the Butcher news."

"Yes."

"Do you know who is in charge?"

"We definitely got a call from your friend in Singapore because they believed you were in danger. It's out of their hands now since he's been spotted here."

"By who?"

"Just a random stranger saw something on the news. He's officially on the America's Most Wanted list so we've been getting some calls but nothing that's led us to him."

"I think he might be in Georgia…. Or headed to Louisiana, or …goddammit, I don't know if he's just a ghost popping up everywhere."

"What's going on Harley?"

"I just got a call from his mother who claims he was outside of her house. She has a patrol car sitting outside of it but who knows if those guys are sleeping on the job."

"It'll cost them their lives if they are."

"No kidding. Can you send guys out there to help?"

"Actually Harley, it's out of our hands now too."

"The FBI?"

"Yeah, they have their hands in it now and we're out entirely."

"Can you give me the contact? I'm heading back to Louisiana myself to make sure Savannah is okay."

"Harley, just stay out of it. I don't want you anywhere near him."

She sighed. "I don't have a choice, Cap. He's called

me twice. I think he's on my tail. Even if I went home, he would just follow me. I have to try to stop him or I'm dead anyways."

"Shit. Okay, the agent in charge is Agent Sheldon Walters. But I'm warning you, he's a dick."

She smiled. "Great."

"He is working with a partner named Agent Riley Dawson. He seems a little more reasonable. They are perched here for the time being."

He rattled off the phone numbers for her and she motioned to Danny to grab her a pen. He handed her a pen with a notepad, and she wrote down the numbers.

"Thanks, Captain."

"Harley, if you need anything and I mean anything, you call me, and I'll do whatever I can. You stay safe. I don't want to lose you to that monster."

"I'll do my best."

She clicked off the call. She looked to the Sheriff. "We have to hit the road again, Sheriff."

"I understand you have your hands full."

"Do me a favor. I would like to stay involved, but I think you need to do some digging into her past. See if she's been married before. If she's had other children."

He paled considerably. "Dear God."

"I'm afraid so. Have one of your guys do a search and call me with the details."

"Will do."

They shook hands with the Sheriff and walked out of the department. Once in the car, Harley just sat in the passenger's seat.

"Are we really heading back to Louisiana?"

"That's the only lead we have, and you told me you weren't scared."

He smiled. "I'm not but that doesn't mean I want to jump into the lion's den."

"I don't either. It's going to be okay."

She said the words, but she didn't believe them for a minute.

FOUR

ON THE DRIVE TOWARDS SAVANNAH'S house, Harley made the call to the FBI agent in charge. She wanted to see if she could help them, but mainly she wanted to know that there was someone else on her side, looking out for her.

She listened to the phone ring.

"Agent Walters."

"Hello Agent, I'm Harley Wolfhart, you might know who I am, but----"

He chuckled, cutting her off. "Yes, Miss. Wolfhart, I know exactly who you are."

She stopped, feeling sheepish. She sometimes forgot that at one point, she was national news. It wasn't every day that someone survived a serial killer.

"Of course, sorry." She laughed. "I was told that you are overseeing the investigation for the Butcher. I thought that I could help."

"I'm not sure how you can help, Harley. We have

a lot of resources at our disposal and don't typically need the aid of some has-been police officer turned private investigator."

Yup, he was an asshole. She was rendered momentarily speechless by his assholic manner.

"Alright, Agent Walter. You don't need my lowly help, I get it. But the Butcher has called me twice and I'm guessing you zero. I'm also on my way to his mother's house in Louisiana where she told me she saw him outside, and I'm guessing you know nothing about that."

There was an epic silence on the other end.

"If you want to help out, Agent, you can meet us there. How about that?" With that, she clicked off the call. She was grinning when she looked over at Danny.

"That was impressive," he said.

"That guy was such a dick! Since when did I become a has-been?"

He laughed. "Is that what he said to you? You're nowhere near a has-been. What you went through and what you did over there in Thailand was legendary."

She blushed. "Thanks."

"You can bet your ass that agent is going to show up in Louisiana now."

She laughed loudly. "Absolutely. Sometimes I wish I would have stayed on the force; I would have had a little more pull."

"I don't blame you for leaving, and now you get to work on the cases you want on your terms."

"I hope we can get back to Savannah before that lunatic does anything to her."

"Do you think he would kill his own mother?"

"Killers like Rayland don't have any sympathy. He has no more feeling for his mother than a random stranger. In fact, I think he hates her. So, it would probably be an easy kill. In fact, I'm confident that he wants to."

"That's so fucked up."

Her phone rang and she groaned. She hoped it wasn't Rayland again. She didn't recognize the number and she clicked on the call.

"Hello?"

"Harley?"

"Yes, who's this?"

"Sheriff Judd."

"Sheriff hello, we just left you an hour ago. Is everything okay?"

"I did what you asked, and I had one of the detectives run a background on Rebecca. She had another family a few years back in Florida. She had a baby, a two-year old." It sounded like the Sheriff was out of breath. "She wasn't married, just a boyfriend. They weren't together long. She doesn't seem to stay in relationships for very long. Her current ex-husband is the only time that she's been married."

"She had another child," Harley said slowly. "She must have been a young mother. What did she do to the baby?"

"She's 33 now. She was in this relationship when

she was 20 and got pregnant right away. The child drowned in the lake behind their house when she was two. Her boyfriend stood by her side and said she could never have hurt the baby. Shockingly enough, she was never a real person of interest. The couple later separated, and she disappeared. She obviously made her way to Georgia where she started over. She met Cindy's father, got married within a year, and then had Cindy a year later, and here we are. The current father is not in the picture. She had these two children all to herself. I talked to her parents. She said she couldn't wait to get out of their house and married the first guy that she could get her hands on. I suspect there might have been some abuse in the home."

Harley tried to absorb the information. It was a lot. Those poor children never stood a chance. She drowned her first child and then she did it again. Why did she keep having children if she didn't want them?

"She's a serial killer." And female serial killers were rare, or harder to catch. She wasn't sure which.

"I've dispatched a couple of deputies to go and pick her up. She was last seen at the hospital trying to see her daughter. She should be easy to find since she loves the cameras. We're going to formally charge her. I'm not taking any chances that she gets in to see her remaining daughter. Wait---hold on Harley, I'm getting another call."

Harley waited wondering if the deputies had already picked up Rebecca.

"Okay, sorry, I'm back."

"No worries, everything okay?"

"She's awake. The eldest daughter is awake."

"Oh my god, that's great."

"I'm heading over there now. She's talking with some difficulty. Her speech was affected. But we might finally know what really happened."

"Well, you might be able to kill two birds with one stone and find the mother there as well."

"Thanks for your help, Harley. I'll keep you posted."

"Thank you and good luck."

She clicked off the call and sighed. Hopefully, that was a case that was quickly closing. She felt for the lone survivor, the child that would have to grow up without her siblings and knowing that her mother had wanted her dead. She wasn't sure how that girl's life was going to get any better, especially without any other family. Who would take care of the poor girl once she left the hospital? There were a million questions that would haunt Harley as she made her way back to Louisiana.

"That woman has killed children before. What is happening to the world that we live in?"

"You know just as well as I do that there have been monsters roaming the earth a lot longer than we have. Unfortunately, this is not a new thing. It sucks to be this close to it but at least it's going to stop now. You helped catch her and make sure that they knew to watch for certain things. She's not going to get away with this and that little girl will be okay, and she'll live to tell what really happened. The mother can't lie her way out of things now."

"I really hope you're right. I hope it's over. We need to get to Savannah now and make sure she's alright. I think we probably should have stayed there and watched over her."

"She had police officers outside her house. It's their job to make sure she's okay. You're only one person. It's not like you were assigned to her."

"I know but you don't know what it was like being on that island and watching each one of my friends get plucked off one by one. It seemed like there was nothing that I could do to stop it."

"Yeah, I get it, but the Butcher is not your average killer. I wouldn't want to be in a room alone with him."

She wasn't the only one that got out of there alive. Her friend Keri had also survived the Butcher and had to go on with her life without her sister and brother-in-law. The Butcher had brutally murdered them while they were on their honeymoon. It had been hard to get Keri off the island before the Butcher had grabbed her too. She had been devastated by the loss of her family and Harley kept meaning to go out to Connecticut to visit her. But with the business up and running and now the Butcher loose, it had been almost impossible to get some time off. Once the Butcher was once again safely behind bars, she would make a point to go and visit Keri and catch up with her. They had bonded over the tragedy and that was one person she didn't want to lose touch with.

When they arrived, there was a patrol car across the street from Savannah's house exactly where Harley expected it to be. Danny had been driving and got out first, with her following soon behind him. They approached the car. Harley could see the deputies inside, coffee in hand, laughing their asses off. Danny tapped on the driver's side window and the deputy sitting there jumped, spilling his coffee. He glared up at Danny while he wound down the window.

"Can I help you?"

"Just wondering what you guys are doing here joking around when there is a serial killer loose. When was the last time that you did a perimeter check?"

"Who the fuck are you?"

"I'm Danny." He motioned to Harley. "This is Harley, you know the same Harley that brought down the Butcher the first time?"

"Miss Wolfhart," they said in awe. Harley wasn't paying attention to them. She was scanning the area. Could the Butcher still be there? Was he watching her? She looked back at the deputies.

"You do realize that Savannah stated that the Butcher was outside of her house? Don't you think that you guys should be paying attention. He's not someone that you want to just stumble upon."

"Oh. I don't think he's here. She was just seeing things. We looked all over the place and there was no sign of him. She's just being paranoid."

"You need to take this seriously."

She walked away. They were as good as dead.

She went up to the house and knocked on the door. When Savannah didn't answer, Harley had a moment of panic rise up. She envisioned bodies piled up. She wasn't sure that she could deal with another of Butcher's reigns of terror.

The door opened and Savannah stood there, but she also didn't. Harley breathed a sigh of relief. Gone was the put-together beauty queen. Her hair was dishevelled, and it looked like she hadn't showered in days. That was not a good sign.

"Savannah, is everything okay?"

"Yes, yes, everything is fine. Come in. I just haven't slept very much since I saw him."

"Are you confident that you saw him?"

"You think I don't know my own son?"

"I'm not saying that. We're just all under a lot of stress right now and you might have just thought you saw him."

"No. He's here and he waved to me. I saw him, he stood there for at least a minute and then walked away. It's not like he appeared in a vision."

"What did he look like?"

"His hair has grown out some and he had a beard.

I guess he didn't clean up since he escaped prison."

Harley couldn't imagine Rayland with a beard, but it made sense. There were pictures of him everywhere at that point and a disguise would be a good idea.

"How would you recognize him," Danny said, always the skeptic. He really didn't like her.

"I know my son. I saw him at the trial. Those eyes could cut through you at any distance. He's here to kill me. I know it."

Harley wasn't sure why Rayland was there. He could have easily killed Savannah by now and didn't. If that's what he wanted, then what was he waiting for? She was starting to feel like this was one big game to him. Maybe it was. Maybe he meant to torture her, spread the fear before he did away with her.

They walked inside her home, and instantly, Harley felt weird. She felt a tingle inside her stomach, and she was immediately on alert. When Savannah stepped into the living room, she almost expected Rayland to jump out at her, but it was empty. She still felt uneasy. Her stomach roiled and she suddenly felt nauseous. Maybe it was the stress of the situation, but she wasn't about to throw up in Savannah's immaculate home.

They sat down on her couch, and she offered them drinks. They declined.

"Would you consider going into protective custody?"

"Absolutely not."

Danny sighed with exasperation. "Savannah, you are convinced that Rayland is here to kill you, but you won't allow us to help you."

"Why can't the two of you just stay here? You can be my guards instead of those two idiots in the front."

"I don't work for the NYPD anymore, Savannah, and I certainly have no jurisdiction in this area. I'm a private investigator now, not a bodyguard. I'm sure now that the FBI is involved, you will have better protection. But I'm advising you to go into protective custody. I'm not sure I would be able to be the best protection for you."

"You would be the perfect person to protect me, Harley."

"She almost died the last time she encountered your son," Danny spat out.

Harley looked at Danny and her gaze softened.

"This is a job for the FBI and from what we've heard, they're already involved. They could be on their way here as we speak. These are the people responsible for your safety. We're here because we want to catch this bastard again. But Harley's safety is just as important as yours. She's in just as much danger as you are."

Savannah just stared at him, speechless.

"Look Savannah, I'm gonna stick around. I'm confident that Rayland is following me, so at this point it's probably best that we all stick together close by. But I am not in charge of this case, and sometime in the very near future, I'm going to be asked to stay out of it. I can do my own investigating but I'm not the person to be your armed guard. I'm sorry."

Savannah just nodded.

"We're going to find a hotel to check into. You have your escorts outside; we'll be back in the morning. I'm going to look into a couple of things in the meantime."

They got up and walked out of the room. When Harley turned, she saw Savannah looking down at the floor and she seemed so small and helpless all of a sudden. The fire had left her. Then a small smile crept across her face and a chill went up Harley's spine.

FIVE

THE BUTCHER WAS ON THE HIGHWAY, traveling. He had stolen a car; one so old it still had a handle to manually wind the windows down. He didn't want to draw any attention to himself and the old, retired couple he stole it from probably wouldn't notice it was missing from the yard for a while.

He had seen Harley at his mother's house, and he knew that it was something that he would have to deal with. But first, he had something that he needed to deal with. As much as he loathed it, he was traveling away from Harley, and it left a void inside of him. She was his match, his soulmate but she didn't see it. If she didn't see it, he would remove her from that world. He would not allow her to exist without him, being pawed by another man. Having another man inside of her. He wouldn't have it. She was his and she wasn't going to get away from him that time.

He pulled into the parking lot of a warehouse. He

shut off the car and sat there in the dark. Nothing moved; the warehouse had been abandoned for years, and he would not be interrupted. He was trying to keep as low of a profile as he could; he was a wanted man, after all. It wouldn't be long before the FBI had his picture splashed over every news station if they hadn't already. Making the America's Most Wanted list was inevitable after what he had done. And he wasn't even close to being finished. The world would bow before him in fear and awe after they saw what he was capable of. Thailand was nothing compared to what he was about to unleash.

He climbed out of the car and made his way to the back where he unlocked the trunk. He stared down at the woman in the truck and smiled. She was bound and gagged, and she shivered as she looked up at him. She recognized him and that filled him with the feeling of joy. He hadn't seen her in months and that little reunion was just the beginning. He closed the trunk again and heard her muffled screams. He needed to make sure that everything was ready before he took her out. He walked inside the warehouse and went down a corridor that led to the warehouse's open space. There would have been a time when the place was filled with pallets of products ready to be shipped out to the masses. But that was no longer the case. Aside from a few boxes and a lot of dust, there wasn't much there. In the middle of the room was a plastic sheet that had a chair in the middle of it. Off to the side, there was a table with his tools. He couldn't get everything that he typically used in these situations, but a power drill and hammer were easily attainable at any hardware store.

The area was quiet, no one would be disturbing him that night. Everything was perfect. He would deal with his past and get back to Harley quickly. She was with his mother, and he couldn't allow that to go on for too long. His mother held some of his deepest secrets and he preferred to keep them secrets.

He quickly made his way back to the vehicle and opened the trunk. He smiled down at his prize and moved to pick her up. The look of terror on her face radiated out of the trunk. She screamed through the tape and the sound made his body hum. There was something bittersweet about tying up loose ends. He slammed his fist into the side of her head, knocking her out. Lifting her out of the trunk, he hoisted her over his shoulder and made his way to his destiny.

SIX

KILL. KILL THEM. I HAD to kill them. I had to try. I had to. No one understands the pressure that I've been under. No one understands what it's like to feel so alone. I thought they were dead. They were all supposed to be dead. I had taken my time. Taken my time to get there. I listened as they cried. I watched the blood come out of Cindy's mouth while she reached for me. I waited. I drove so slowly. Their cries turned into silence, and I thought they were gone to heaven. Heaven was where those sweet babies belonged. They were better off there. But Cindy was still alive, and I hadn't expected that. She can't be allowed to talk. If she tells. No, she would never tell. She loves me. She loves her mother. She will protect me. But first I need to talk to her. Make sure she understands otherwise.... something might happen.

Rebecca sat in her car outside of the hospital. It had been two days since that woman cop told her that her daughter was awake. God knows what those cops were saying to her. She needed to get inside. She knew there was a guard outside the hospital room but so far, they had still allowed her to see her child. But there was no privacy. There was no way for her to make Cindy understand that some secrets needed to be kept.

I would do anything for him. He doesn't like kids. I don't know why he doesn't like kids. He never really talked to me about his childhood. I tried to tell him that they were good little kids and that they wouldn't bother him any. I could keep them on the opposite side of the house and make them be quiet. But he said no. He didn't want to be a daddy. She couldn't let him go. She thought she could. She even tried for a while. But she couldn't stop thinking about him. She needed him in her life. He was the only one who loved her. He was the only man that she had ever loved. She had to do whatever it took to get him back.

She got out of the car, the one that her parents had leant her. Her own vehicle was still being processed as a crime scene. She wasn't sure when she would be getting it back. She hoped that the seats weren't ruined from all that blood. It was a brand-new car and she had just gotten it. She couldn't afford another one. It had to last.

She shut the car door behind her and walked across the parking lot, feeling nervous and self-conscious. She fidgeted as she walked into the entrance of the hospital and made her way into the elevator. Her daughter's room was on the fifth floor and that was where she got out. She walked past the nurse's station when one called out to her.

"Miss. Mayers. Wait, Miss. Mayers. Where are you going?"

"To see my daughter, of course," she said while still walking towards the room.

"You can't go in there."

Rebecca swung around. "You can't keep me from my own child. I haven't done anything wrong, and I haven't been arrested."

She turned and walked away from the nurse and made her way down the hall. There was an officer standing outside her door.

"I'm here to see my daughter, get out of my way."

The officer let her pass, but he followed her into the room.

Cindy was awake when she went in, and her eyes grew wide. Rebecca moved to the side of her against the bed.

"Oh, my precious Cindy. We'll be getting out of here soon and then you'll be coming back home with me. It'll just be the two of us now, but that's okay, right?" She turned towards the officer. "I thought she was in a coma. Why didn't anyone tell me that she was awake?"

"Ma'am, why haven't you been here to check on her? Or called the hospital. If you don't know anything that's not my fault."

Rebecca turned back to her daughter, gushing all over her. Cindy just stared back at her. She hated the fact that there was a cop watching her the entire time. Wasn't she allowed some privacy with her own child?

She bent in close to Cindy's ear and whispered. "I'll get you out of here soon, Cindy. I love you so much. I *love* you, Cindy. Do you understand?"

"Miss. Mayers, what are you doing here?"

She turned to see Sheriff Judd entering the room. She stood up from the bed. "I want your officers to stay out of the hospital. There is no need for them to be here harassing Cindy all the time. Trying to force her to talk when she needs time to heal. How is she supposed to get any better with you guys hounding her all the time?"

"The officers stay."

She blanched. "How do you think it makes me feel having to come in here and be watched with my own child? Like I'm some kind of criminal. I want to spend some time privately with Cindy without having officers and nurses listening to everything I say. That's not right."

Sheriff Judd stared down at her, his face expressionless. "The officers stay.

"I'm going to have my lawyer kick all of you out of here. You're harassing her."

"You can sure try, but any judge is going to vote in favor of the child's best interest, and as long as there is an investigation, we are going to protect her."

"Protect her from who? I'm certainly not going to hurt her."

"We're going to protect her from whoever shot her. That person could walk in here any day and try to finish the job. You wouldn't want that would you?"

She seethed with rage, and she wanted nothing more than to wipe the smirk off his face. Who the hell did he think he was?

Her face was beet red. "You're going to pay for this."

She turned back to Cindy. "I'll come back and visit you again, sweetheart when it's not so crowded in here. I love you."

The heart rate monitor was beeping uncontrollably. She turned and walked out of the room, leaving the rest of them standing there. She walked down the hall, past the nurse's station, refusing to acknowledge them. They must have called the Sheriff. All they were doing was trying to cause trouble for her.

She was back sitting in her car, shaking with rage. These people were getting in her way of what she wanted. She couldn't believe that Cindy was still alive. She had driven so slowly. So very slow. She didn't understand how it had all happened. She had planned so meticulously and now there was one still alive.

She jumped when there was a knock on her window. Startled, she expected to see Sheriff Judd at the window. He had been breathing down her neck, trying to make her feel guilty. Like she had done something wrong, and she had nothing to feel guilty about. She deserved to be happy too, didn't she? No one had ever asked her what would make her happy? They just expected her to go along with their plans. She was tired of it. She was in love, and she wanted to spend her life with him.

She stared out the window, realizing that it wasn't the sheriff at the window. She pressed the button to lower her window.

She couldn't believe her eyes. He looked so different.

"I've seen you on TV. The Butcher."

The man curled his lips into a smile.

SEVEN

HARLEY WOKE UP IN THE hotel room, rolling over in the plush sheets. The bed was damn comfortable, she almost didn't want to get out of bed. She didn't have a choice; however, her phone was buzzing, and if it continued, it would buzz its way right off the side table. Groaning, she sat up and rubbed at her eyes. She picked up the phone, checking the time. 7am.

"What the hell," she moaned.

She clicked on the call. "Hello," she grumbled into the phone.

"Harley, it's Sheriff Judd."

She sat up in the bed. Something was wrong.

"Sheriff, is everything okay?"

"I have good news and bad news, Harley."

"Just give me the bad news, I'm used to it at this point."

"We lost the mother."

A chill ran up her spine. "You don't mean Rebecca, I hope?"

"Unfortunately, yes. She's gone. Disappeared."

"What happened?"

"We're not really sure. The little girl woke up, and we've questioned her, but she's mute. Absolutely terrified. We're guessing she's worried her mother is going to come looking for her. Rebecca had gotten in her room one night and was trying to talk to her. At this point, we can't take our chance that Rebecca's lawyer won't get permission to see the child. So, we're just going to arrest her and take our chances. We believe it will only be a matter of time before the girl will talk. We just need to get her to trust us. Maybe you can talk to her yourself."

"God, Sheriff, I'm up to my arms in bullshit. I can't make any promises, but I'll try to come. I just need to be here for a few days to see how things are going to pan out. If I can get some protection for Savannah, I might be able to catch an overnight flight just to come and talk. We haven't had any action over here in the past two days so maybe he won't be coming back this way."

"The girl is a mess. Totally understandable, but we need to get her to admit what happened."

"She must have known that you were coming for her, and she fled the state."

"No, I don't think so. She saw her daughter the one time, but she told us that she was going to get her lawyer after us. She never did come back to the hospital and that was days ago. She hasn't done any interviews. No one has seen her. I think her fleeing the state would have been premature. It hasn't even been reported by the media. We're not sure what happened to her after that interview."

"So where did she go then? This is all a little odd."

"She disappeared, Harley. Up in smoke. She's not doing interviews, she's not at the hospital. We've checked her home. There is no sign of her."

She swallowed hard, suddenly feeling a little ill. "Hold that thought." Harley ran to the bathroom and pushed open the door, collapsing before the toilet. She vomited inside, emptying what little she had in her stomach. She dry heaved into the toilet until nothing else came up. She wiped at her mouth and climbed from her spot. Washing her hands, she looked in the mirror. What the hell was that? The stress of it all was getting to her. The thought that Rayland was hunting her, watching her, was all a little too much to take.

She returned to her phone. "Sorry, Sheriff."

"Is everything okay?"

"Yes, I haven't been feeling well."

"I'm sorry to be bothering you. But this is all out of our comfort zone. We've never dealt with a serial killer before."

"What is going to happen to the little girl?"

"She's going to be okay. We are going to do everything we can to get her some therapy. We have a wonderful foster home set up for her. A really good family that's looking to adopt. Of course, the only way that adoption can even be considered is if she's convicted. Otherwise, that poor kid goes back to live with her mother."

"That poor child."

"She'll be okay. She's much better off now that she's away from her mother. It's a miracle she survived to begin with."

"Yes. I know. Keep me posted, Sheriff, if she turns up."

Harley clicked off the call and hurried around the hotel room getting ready for the day. When she finished, she left and went to the next doorway in the hall. She knocked, hoping that Danny was already up. He answered the door in grey sweatpants. She averted her eyes immediately. "Get your ass ready, I need coffee."

He smirked as she turned from him and made her way downstairs to wait for him. She was in the lobby when he finally made his way down.

"Where's the fire, Harley? I was in the middle of watching a Tik Tok video of a parade of ducks."

She smiled. "I was ripped out of my sleep as well so we might as well get on with the day."

They drove to the nearest coffee shop and sat in one of the booths. Danny went to the counter to get them coffee while she scrolled through the news in Georgia on her phone. She didn't see anything about the child waking up in the hospital just like the Sheriff said. She also didn't find anything regarding Rebecca or her whereabouts. Where could she have gone? It didn't make any sense.

Danny sat down across from her. "What's on your mind?"

"Sheriff called this morning. Rebecca is missing. Gone without a trace."

"What? How?"

"I don't know but I have a really bad feeling about it."

"What do you mean?"

"We're missing something here. I'm missing something. The girl is awake, but she's not talking. He wants me to come down and see if I can help convince her."

"That's a lot. We can't keep going back and forth. It's not exactly down the street. As much as I want to get involved in Georgia. We can't focus on that. The sheriff knows what he's doing. We have the Butcher in our backyard and who knows how close he is. We have bigger things to worry about."

"You're right. If I keep this going, I'm going to be murdered in my sleep because I wasn't paying attention to Butcher. There's just something up with that woman, the fact that she's missing. It's going to haunt me."

"Maybe she decided to get outta dodge. Her lawyer could have told her she fucked up and she got scared."

"It doesn't feel right."

"None of this feels right." He laughed. "To be honest, when you hired me, I thought I was going to be tracking down cheating husbands and now I've met one serial killer, and I could meet another."

"Having regrets?"

He smiled. "No. But I have a feeling my life is going to be far more interesting. I don't think that you need to be Savannah's protector though. She's not your responsibility. I'm not even sure that we should stay here. Maybe we go back home and hire you some bodyguards. We might be too close here."

"No, you're right. I do feel that staying close to her is the best way to get close to Butcher. But the FBI are involved now, so I don't need to be here for her. But it's also the safest place for me, for all of us. We're creating an army here, rather than me being alone in New York."

"You wouldn't be alone."

She smiled. "You know what I mean." She took a sip of her coffee and watched as her phone light up. It was her old Captain.

"That's weird."

"What is it?"

She picked up her phone. "It's my old boss. What could he want?"

She clicked on the call. "Captain. What's up?"

There was a beat of silence and she wondered if the call had been disconnected.

"Captain?"

"Harley, sorry. I have some bad news."

A sliver of dread burrowed deep within her gut. It seemed like every time the phone rang, she expected bad news.

"What is it?"

"God, Harley, I don't know how to tell you this."

"For God's sake, *just* tell me."

"It's Keri."

Harley's stomach turned. "No, please, no."

"Her body was found in her apartment this morning by her mother. Just her body was found. Just her body."

Harley's hand went to her mouth as tears rolled down her cheeks. Danny was looking at her alarmed. She couldn't keep eye contact with him, her vision blurred from the tears.

"He said that he was cleaning up loose ends. It never occurred to me that he meant he was going after the survivors of the island."

"He's still calling you?"

"Well, I haven't heard from him in a bit. I guess I now know why. He was seen at his mother's home and then he disappeared. He must have gone after Keri. Oh my god, what she's gone through already. She must have been so scared." She was sobbing now, and Danny got up from his chair, standing awkwardly beside her. She felt like she was going to be sick. Her head spun dizzily as she thought about the Butcher claiming her friend's head as a prize. Where had he put it? Did he have it with him?

"I'm sorry, Harley. I know she meant a lot to you. We should have sent her protection, but it didn't occur to me either that he would go after her. We thought he was after you."

"He is after me, he's trying to hurt me. He had no reason at all to go after her. She wasn't a threat to him in any way and she didn't live close to any of us. For him to travel all that way was an attack on me. I think he's planning on killing his mother. But we don't know when. Who knows when he'll strike again."

Poor Keri. Her eyes filled with tears. Tears that seemed to flow endlessly. She had just spoken to her a week ago. She should have taken her up on that visit. Maybe she would have been there at the right time to help her. She thought that Keri was safe once she was off the island. She thought that they were all safe but that wasn't the case at all. They were just as vulnerable there than they were on the island because there was a monster loose. He was going to take down all of them. Who were the loose ends left from the island? Harley. She was the last one left alive. Harley knew that whatever death Keri endured it was slow and terrifying. That was the last thing that Harley wanted. She thought that she was safe, and she had failed her once again. Aside from Deputy Ned, everyone on that island that she spent time with was dead. Their heads were removed from their bodies and showcased as souvenirs.

"Harley, what the hell is going on?"

She looked up at Danny, forgetting that he was even there.

"Harley, I can send help your way. Fuck the FBI, I don't care how many of them are involved. I'm willing to send some of our team to help you out. Protect you.

I think you need an army around you."

She was shaking her head, but nothing was coming out of her mouth. She felt physically ill. She dropped the phone and ran to the bathroom. Pushing the bathroom door open, she collided with a woman coming out.

"I'm sorry," muttered Harley as the woman cursed at her. She flung herself into a stall, not even locking the door. She bent down at the toilet and threw up. She retched and retched until she had nothing left in her stomach. What was the matter with her? After the things that she saw on the island, she shouldn't be so sensitive to the gore that the Butcher created. Things were getting out of hand again, but it was nothing that she hadn't already seen before. Her head spun dizzily, and she slowly got up from her crouched position before the toilet. She left the stall and went to the sink. She washed her hands and rinsed out her mouth. Her throat burned from throwing up. She looked at herself in the mirror. She had bags under her eyes and her skin was pale. She wasn't getting as much sleep as she would like, but that was expected when you had a serial killer hunting you. She hadn't been feeling the best, but that could just be the stress. They had been traveling back and forth between states so it wasn't unexpected that she would feel a little worn out.

She dried her hands and left the bathroom. Danny watched her as she approached the table. He watched silently as he drank his coffee.

Harley looked down at the phone on the table.

"I finished the call for you. He's really concerned about you, Harley but I told him that the FBI was involved, so he would probably be wasting his time sending men down. He could always send some later if the FBI was open to it, but they won't be."

She nodded and slid into her seat. She took her coffee in her hands and just stared into it. Too much too soon seemed to be the theme of her life. When she started her business, she hadn't expected things to get so dramatic so quickly.

"I'm sorry, Harley. I didn't know her but it's pretty obvious the news rocked you. You met her on the island?"

It was hard to swallow past the lump in her throat. It was still hard to grasp that Keri was gone in such a horrendous way. Harley felt responsible for her. She had underestimated the Butcher and what he was capable of. No one was safe.

"Yes, she was there with her sister and brother-in-law. They were newlyweds. I had met them as a bigger group. I was seeing someone on the island, and these were his friends. I spent a few weeks with them before the killings started. Keri and her sister were so close, obviously close enough to go on vacation with them. The couple was madly in love. They were on their honeymoon and to lose her family like that was horrific. She was still dealing with that, and for him to go after her again is so fucked up. She had to find out that her sister and husband were beheaded. I can't imagine what she must have gone through with the Butcher. The fear, and pain she must have experienced being in his clutches. Why couldn't he have just come for me?"

"He is Harley. This is all part of it. He's hurting you as much as he can. You know that this is some kind of game for him. And I wouldn't wish for him to come for you any sooner than he's planning on it. That's inevitable, Harley. He's coming for you whether he would have got Keri or not. He's not finished here."

She put her head in her hands. "I know." She groaned.

"Are you doing, okay? You seem to be getting sick a lot. It's not like you. I mean I don't know how I would feel if a serial killer was after me. But I never took you for the sensitive type."

She laughed. "I'm not but it's been a hell of a week."

Harley's phone rang. It was Savannah. She picked it up.

"Harley, the FBI are here."

Harley smiled. "We'll be right over."

She clicked off the call and looked at Danny. "We're up."

EIGHT

SAVANNAH'S HOME HAD THE AMBIANCE of a coffin as they pulled up. Harley shuddered, looking at the house that was now surrounded by multiple black SUVs. Why did they have to buy the same vehicles? It was so ominous. She got out of the car and looked across the roof at Danny as he got out.

"Don't expect any type of cooperation from these guys. They're going to tell us to pack up and go," he said.

She smirked. "Oh, trust me, we'll be using them more than they'll be using us."

"Thatta girl!" He said laughing. They walked up to the door and knocked. It was seconds before Savannah flung open the door.

"What are they doing here?" She practically screeched.

Harley sighed as she walked inside the home. "Savannah, we told you that the FBI was going to arrive. It's out of my hands. But having the FBI protecting you is not a bad thing. Relax, it's going to be a long day." She walked into the living room with Danny behind her. The agents were sitting on the couch looking over files. They both had a fresh glass of sweet tea beside them, condensation collecting on the glass. They looked up when she came in the room. They were close to the same age, both in their mid-thirties. One had longish dark hair and a lean build. When he smiled, his whole face brightened up and his green eyes practically glowed. She guessed that it was Agent Riley Dawson, the friendly one.

"I'm surprised that you are still here," Agent Sheldon Walters grumbled.

"I'm surprised you showed up at all. I thought you would have had the Butcher in cuffs by now," she said dryly. "Oh, wait. You guys haven't caught him yet?"

Danny smirked while the agent glared at her.

Agent Dawson got up from the couch and walked over to her. "Miss Wolfhart, it's an absolute pleasure meeting you."

She smiled at him. He was easy on the eyes. She could at least tolerate him while the FBI was there.

"If you think for a minute we need your help Harley, you can save your breath."

She looked past Agent Dawson and stared at the other FBI agent.

"He killed my friend last night. Trust me, you need me a hell of a lot more than I need you."

Agent Walters got up from the couch and threw his

file across the room. "Goddammit, how the fuck does she know more about this case than I do?"

She smiled.

"Hey, watch how you talk to her," Danny cautioned. "Harley has always been a valuable asset to this case and you're a moron if you think otherwise."

"Who the fuck brought the giant?" Agent Walters glowered at him.

Harley was holding back a smile. "He works for me, Agent, and I'm not going anywhere, so I suggest you get used to it. What would be nice is if we all started to work together on this. The Butcher is out there, and he's started killing again. How many do you want on his death toll this time?"

Agent Dawson put up his hand. "Look Harley, you're right. We have a psychopath on our hands and the best way for us to catch him is to start working together. He's been here once, he's likely to come back again."

"I think Harley needs to leave. She's a liability." Agent Walters wasn't giving up. "The only people dying, are people you know."

Ouch. Harley glared at the agent.

"She needs to stay here," screamed Savannah and Harley jumped. The room stilled and everyone turned to face Savannah. The woman swallowed hard and cleared her throat. "I mean—I just feel safer with her here. She's the only one that survived him. She knows him better than all of you."

Harley narrowed her eyes at Savannah. Something

was off about her, but she couldn't put her finger on what it was.

"Alright, that settles it then." Agent Dawson stated. He turned and started picking up the papers from the file that Walters tossed. He set the file on the table and turned back to Harley. "Tell us about the murder."

"My Captain called me this morning, not even an hour ago. I guess he's my old Captain now." She took a deep breath and let it out slowly. "It was Keri, one of the survivors from the island."

"Good god," Savannah whispered behind her.

"I had talked to her a couple of weeks ago. Just small talk but there's a chance that Rayland knew that. He's called me multiple times; I know he's here. One of the times that he called me he mentioned that he needed to start tying up loose ends. I thought he meant his mother. So, we rushed here, especially after she said that she had seen him outside of her house. It never occurred to me that he was going after Keri. I thought she was safe."

Riley was staring at her intently. His eyes glistened briefly, and he nodded. "I'm sorry about your loss Harley, but you have to know that it's not your fault. Everything is psychological with these guys. They know how to get to you, how to manipulate you."

"She died because of me."

"Maybe so. But that's not your fault and there wasn't a thing that you would have been able to do to stop it. You're not a mind reader."

"I should have been able to anticipate where he was going to go next."

"As much as you would like to think so, Harley, you're not superhuman. I don't think that any of us would have anticipated that move. We all thought she was safe. It's best that you try not to save lives at this point because you're the one with a target on your back. He's here for you, and we all know that."

Danny jumped in. "I think it was pretty obvious that he had you focus on his mother so that you wouldn't consider anyone else in danger."

That was true. She hadn't thought about the fact that Rayland had orchestrated the whole thing. The moment that Savannah called her and told her that Rayland was there. Harley had made sure that she was there. She wanted to avoid anymore losses. She wouldn't always know who he was going after, but she thought protecting Savannah was a good bet.

"We can only guess at this point, but I would bet any dollar amount that he'll be calling Harley soon. He will be coming for her, and we need to be prepared for that." Danny said, his brow furrowed. He was worried. She should probably be worried, too, since she was his target, but she was just so angry. She felt it deep within her bones. She had been unable to kill him on the island and now he was back killing people that mattered to her. She felt nauseous again and hoped she was going to get sick in front of anyone.

"I need some air."

"Are you okay?" Dawson asked.

"Yes, I'm just going to run to the store. Get some supplies. Where are you guys staying tonight?"

"You all need to stay here. Especially you Harley." Savannah said, her voice a shrill.

Shocked Harley stared at her. Savannah blinked a couple of times. "I mean…. I don't want to be alone."

Agent Walter was still staring at Savannah when he cleared his throat uncomfortably. "We are stationed at a hotel in town."

"Yes, so are we, but if you have the room, Savannah, me and Danny could hunker down here for the night in case Rayland calls."

Savannah smiled faintly.

"Well maybe it's best that we all stay here just for the night. It's very likely that the Butcher will call, and we might be able to get a read on him. Trace the call." Dawson added.

With pursed lips, Savannah said, "I will start making up some beds." Harley watched her leave the room and then she headed for the front door.

"Harley, I don't think you should be going anywhere alone."

"I don't think that he's gonna snatch me in the aisle at Walgreens. I won't be long."

She turned and left without another word. She closed the front door behind her and breathed in the fresh air. She still felt a little ill and she made a mental note to grab some Pepto Bismol. She couldn't risk being sick now, there was too much to do. She got into the SUV and started it. She looked around the neighbourhood, scanning the yards and the homes, checking the sidewalks.

"Where are you Rayland?" She whispered.

He could already be there, or he could be miles away. There was no way to know, not until he decided to show himself. He was holding all the cards, and they were just pawns in his game. She pulled away from the house and drove. She checked her rearview mirror to see if anyone pulled out into the street behind her. The closest drug store was about a block away and she periodically checked her mirrors until she pulled into the parking lot. She hadn't been alone in a week, and it was nice to have a moment, her thoughts her own.

She perused the aisles until she found the Pepto Bismol. She grabbed a box and then grabbed some ibuprofen. She continued down the aisles, picking up things that she thought she might need over the next few days. She stopped in one aisle and stared at the products on the shelf. She sighed as she pulled a box off the shelf and put it in her basket. She was hoping she wasn't going to have to use it.

She left the drugstore and was almost at the SUV when her phone rang. Thinking it was Danny, she answered it without looking at who it was.

"Hello, beautiful."

A chill ran up her spine. She could barely swallow. She just stood there in the parking lot frozen. Her eyes darted around the parking lot, sure that he was going to be standing there waiting for her. *You just had to go to the store alone, didn't you?*

"Harley, are you there?"

She finally found her voice. "Rayland, where are you?"

"Do you really expect me to make things easy on you? We'll meet again when it's the right time."

"I'm going to kill you for what you did to Keri."

"C'mon now. Her time was up in Thailand. I would have had her sooner had you not got in the way."

"Fuck you."

"Now is that any way to talk to an old friend?"

"We're not friends."

"No, we used to be a lot more. Those are some of my fondest memories. Those nights in your hotel room kept me warm at night while I rotted in prison."

She shuddered. "You got what you deserved, and I'll put you back there if I don't kill you first."

"I'll be seeing you real soon, Harley."

With that, the call went dead, and she dropped her hand to her side. Her heart hammered in her chest as she hurried to the vehicle.

NINE

"YOU HAVE TO BE SHITTIN' me."

"What the hell is your problem, Sheldon?"

He was sneering at Harley. "I just find it convenient that you snuck out of here and that's when the Butcher decides to call you."

"Fuck you. What do you think, he and I are working together? That would really be something."

"I've seen worst things happen in my career; it certainly wouldn't be the first time."

"Whoa, whoa, Sheldon, dammit, this isn't helping." Riley stepped in between them.

Harley was standing in the middle of Savannah's kitchen arguing with Agent Walters. She had arrived back from the drugstore and let them know that Rayland had called her. She hadn't expected to be attacked, however, and she was about sick and tired of working with the FBI.

"We're all on the same team here. Harley isn't working

with the Butcher, that's absolutely crazy. I think we're all just getting frustrated that we have no leads on him. At this point, the guy is a ghost."

She glared at Agent Walters. She was close to getting in her vehicle and heading back to New York. She was there to help, and she was only getting railroaded by an agent who was three fries short of a Happy Meal. It was then that she realized that Danny wasn't there defending her. She looked around the room.

"Where's Danny?"

It immediately put a stop to the conversation. Agent Walters threw his hands up in the air. Harley ignored him.

"Oh, he went to your hotel."

"What for?"

"He wanted to make sure you had your things for the evening. I'm not sure if he's checking out or just grabbing your things. He said he wanted to grab some of his things and your bags. You also have some files there?"

"I wish he would have waited for me. Why didn't one of you go with him?"

Agent Walters smirked. "He's a pretty big guy. I don't think he needs a babysitter."

"The men that died on the island were also well-built men and that didn't stop the Butcher."

"I'm sure he's fine." Agent Dawson muttered. "He seems to be a detail-oriented guy. Are you two involved?"

Her mouth dropped open. "Absolutely not."

"I didn't mean to offend you. He's just very protective of you."

"I think that's a natural inclination for any man, or at least it should be."

Agent Dawson blushed. "Of course."

She turned and went into the kitchen to get something to drink. She walked in on Savannah who was talking on a landline in the kitchen. She wasn't aware that Harley had entered the room because she had her back to her.

"I told you that I would do as you asked…. yes… I told you I would…everything is going as planned…." Savannah looked over her shoulder and gasped. She hung up the phone quickly. Eyebrows raised; Harley stared at her.

"What do you think you're doing, sneaking up on people?"

"I didn't even know you were in here, Savannah. I just came in for a drink."

"Well, you scared me to death."

"I'm sorry about that," she said calmly. "Who were you talking to?"

"Just some family. They don't like that I have police in my home. They're a little worried."

Harley stared at her. Savannah fidgeted.

"If you would like, I can talk to them. I can help to make them feel comfortable that we're here to protect you, not to hurt you."

She waved her off. "Nonsense, there is no need for that. They were just checking in with me. I can take care of myself."

Savannah walked out of the room. Harley stood in the middle of the kitchen, a chill running up her spine. Did she hear what she thought she heard on the phone? Could it be explained away?

She needed to talk to Danny. She pulled out her phone and texted him.

Where are you? If you go to Starbucks without bringing me something back, I'll kill you.

She put her phone away and left the kitchen.

TEN

THE BUTCHER WAS DRIVING DOWN a back road looking for an address. He knew where he had to be and what he needed to do. He had a plan and the steps to completing that plan had been implemented. It was going to be his greatest work. He always planned about ten steps ahead. He had been doing it his whole life. That was how he had managed to stay undetected for so long. It didn't hurt that he had a background in security. He had stashes of passports and cash in multiple locations. That was how he was able to leave Thailand so easily and quickly. He was able to go to an undisclosed location, grab a new identity and get on an airplane before the police even knew that he was gone. He had plenty of money so moving from place to place was never difficult. He had no intention of returning to the Singapore prison, once his work was finished in the United States, he would head to Spain to start over.

He looked to his right and a beautiful woman sat

beside him. She wasn't a potential victim. Instead, she might just be his soulmate. He had never met another woman who had a soul as dark as his was. She killed children, she might be even darker than him. He had never met anyone like her. Usually, he had to deal with hiding himself from people, putting on a mask so no one could see who he really was. But not with her. Her soul was like an oil slick, and she didn't have an ounce of emotion to her. She had willingly killed her children and she hadn't shed a tear over it.

She smiled back at him, a sultry look that caused a stir in his loins. Her darkness aroused him, and he would make use of her body the first chance that he got.

"You need to show your loyalty to me."

Her smile widened. "I'll do anything for you."

"Kill for me then."

She simply nodded. He knew exactly who he was going to let her practice on.

"It's time."

After acquiring a rental in the middle of nowhere thanks to his new lady's credentials, Butcher and Rebecca entered the cabin. Everything was set into place and the plan was underway. It took a lot of effort to get an unconscious Danny into the cabin, but between the two of them, they got through it. He had started to wonder if they would need a forklift, but in the end, Danny was perched unconscious on a kitchen chair. The setup was standard practice for the Butcher. Plastic on the floor, masking tape, a saw, a couple of different drills and garbage bags. He had picked up his favorite whiskey and Rebecca had a playlist on her phone so that he could listen to Beethoven's *Fur Elise* while he worked.

He imagined they weren't going to get their security deposit back on the cabin and he smiled as he imagined what the owners would think if they had any idea what was about to transpire. Things were different now, more dangerous. The Butcher was playing an entirely different game, and no one would be left alive that time. Once he cleaned up the mess he made in the United States, he would head back overseas where he could once again disappear. He glanced at Rebecca who was now sitting across from Danny. She was mocking him, playing with him. She made him smile. He hadn't decided yet if he would keep her around for very long. It could be fun to see the damage they could get into together. Maybe he would take her with him when he traveled to Spain.

She got up and moved slowly towards him. She had a way about her that was entirely mysterious. He could look at her expression but had no idea what was going on in her head. He knew one thing; she was just as likely to kill you as kiss you. Anyone who could take the life of their own child was capable of anything. She was nightmare fuel wrapped in a stunning package.

She stood before him and gazed into his eyes. Her mouth was on his in seconds. He grew hard quickly and drew her closer to him. She started pulling off her clothing and her shirt and brought the zipper down on her jeans slowly as if teasing him. He grinned as he watched her. At the very least Rebecca was a trip, one that he was fully willing to take. He glanced at Danny who was now awake and struggling against his restraints. He stopped and stared at them in disbelief. The Butcher stared back at him as he unzipped his pants, watching as Rebecca got down on her knees.

Danny sat frozen in the chair the moment he looked into the eyes of the Butcher. They had him tied up in an old living room lounge chair. It was sturdy and the arms thick with the rope tied around his arms. He stared at the knots wondering if the Butcher had ever been a sailor. He looked around the home, not recognizing anything. Whose house was it and how far away from the hotel was he?

He was still trying to process how he arrived in that place when the two of those animals started taking off their clothes. He stared in shock as they undressed before him, taking their time, not worried in the least that someone might stumble upon their kidnapping scene. He shook his head, trying to clear the fog in his brain. They must have drugged him with something.

When the Butcher and his concubine started writhing on the floor together, something snapped in his brain. There was no doubt in his mind that he was going to die. He had totally underestimated the Butcher. Danny had believed the Butcher was just your run-of-the-mill psychopath, but he had been wrong, so very wrong. The Butcher was completely and terrifyingly insane, and now there were two of them. He had watched them undress and perform various sex acts in front of him as if he didn't exist. Who does that? He stared down at the floor that the chair was sitting on, noticing the plastic. He swallowed hard. He had been worried about Harley going out alone and never considered the option that someone else might be the target. One minute, he was throwing their suitcases into the back of the SUV, and the next, he saw blackness. They must have hit him from behind. No wait, it was that needle in his neck. It creeped him out wondering how long they had been following him. When he woke up, he realized that the Butcher had acquired a new friend. His blood had turned to ice when he first saw Rebecca with him.

He couldn't figure out how the two had found each other. Had they always been working together? If so, what were the chances that Harley got called in to advise on the case? Was the Butcher's reach really that far?

The Butcher and Rebecca were lying together on the living room couch as if they were a newly romantic couple, trying to discover as much about each other as they could. It was the most surreal experience in his life, and he wondered if he was dreaming. He had to be, right? It couldn't be real being in the room with those two acting like they were falling in love while he was tied to the chair waiting to see what they were going to do to him. The truth was, he knew exactly what they were going to do to him. He tried not to think about the articles he had read about Harley and the Butcher. It was straight out of a horror movie, and it was the last thing that he should be thinking about at that moment. If he dwelled on it, he would go crazy.

He squeezed against the restraints, hoping something other than his mind would snap. Just when he thought it couldn't get worse, the new couple started making out again until they were locked once again in a lustful embrace. His stomach rolled as they started having sex in front of him again. He was losing hope by the second because he realized rather quickly that he was surrounded by madness and there wasn't a soul in the world who knew where he was. The thing that terrified him the most was that they weren't worried at all. They weren't working at a hurried pace to get the job done. It was like they had all the time in the world to kill him and they probably did. Who would find him there? He didn't even know whose home they were in. Was it Rebecca's? Was he still in New Orleans?

Once satiated, the two stopped whispering amongst each other. It was Rebecca that turned to him first and a chill went up his spine when she looked at him. She was analyzing him, reading him. He was easily twice her size but there was nothing he could do about it in that chair. The Butcher was watching her reaction to Danny. He was enjoying every moment of it. She would do the dirty work because the Butcher was always in control. Danny stretched against his restraints knowing that it was futile. He felt weaker than he was like his strength had its limits. What the hell did they drug him with? *And who in the hell put on classical music?*

"There is no use struggling, Danny. I've been doing this a long time, and no one has escaped my restraints. I've made sure that despite your monstrous size, you're not going anywhere. I also have more to administer to you if I need to."

Danny pressed against the back of the chair in the hopes of tipping it over only to receive a smile from the Butcher. He walked over to Danny and removed the gag. Danny knew there was no point in begging for his life. The Butcher had no soul.

"It's a remote cabin, screaming is futile. I've been watching you for awhile, Danny. You shouldn't have gotten yourself involved with Harley."

Danny stopped struggling and made eye contact with the killer. "You sick son of a bitch. You're in love with her, aren't you? Do you think that if you eliminate all the men around her, she'll come back to her, you fucking monster? I just work for her; I'm not involved with her. I have a girlfriend." He choked on the last word, suddenly worried that the Butcher would go and find her.

Rebecca's head snapped toward The Butcher; he ignored her. Something flashed in the Butcher's eyes. It was gone as soon as it came but Danny knew he was right. Which meant that Harley was in far worse danger than he thought. He wasn't going to be able to protect her.

"He's just trying to get under your skin, love. Just ignore him. He doesn't know how connected we are." He turned to her. "Once we deal with him, we will go find your daughter before we deal with Harley together."

"Your daughter? Just leave her alone. Haven't you done enough to your poor family?"

Rebecca smiled. "I gave them life. They belong to me."

Danny stared at her. He didn't know what to say. There was no arguing with psychopaths. He could beg for the lives of her children, but she didn't feel a thing. There would be nothing that he could say that would make a bit of difference to her.

"Rayland, we're just wasting time here," she whispered.

He nodded. "Yes, you're right. Let's get on with it then."

Danny watched him walk to a table placed against the fireplace. He hadn't noticed the tools set up on the table. His head started to spin. Rebecca followed the Butcher and the two of them giggled together at the table. Rebecca picked up an electric saw and Danny's vision started to swim. His skin broke out in goose flesh. The Butcher stood back as she approached him, with a smile on his face as if he was watching a prized student out in the world for the first time. He steeled himself, refusing to beg for his life.

When she turned the saw on, he thought he might start screaming but when the saw connected with his skin, the screams became part of the home.

ELEVEN

HARLEY PACED THE KITCHEN IN Savannah's home. The agents were sitting at the dining room table. There had been no further word from the Butcher, nor was there progress on the case. They didn't have any idea where to start because he just kept moving around literally from state to state. The only confidence they had was knowing that he would one day come for Harley, it was just a matter of time.

"How could you guys let him go alone?"

Agent Walters scoffed. "For God's sake, Harley. The man is over six feet; he wasn't asking for a bodyguard. Even you demanded to go to the store alone. He can take care of himself. We can't babysit everyone."

She shook her head. "No. Something is wrong. It shouldn't be taking this long."

"Okay, let's go check the hotel." Agent Dawson got up from the table. He pulled his keys from his pocket. "We'll make sure he's okay. We're not getting anything accomplished here anyway." He turned to his partner. "You can stay behind and watch out for Savannah."

Sheldon grumbled but agreed.

Harley smiled gratefully and they both headed toward the door.

Harley's heart was thundering in her chest when she pulled up to the SUV in the parking lot of the hotel. There was a suitcase lying on its side on the ground behind the SUV. The trunk was left hanging open.

"Shit."

She pulled into the parking spot beside the SUV. Agent Dawson got out. "I'll go inside and check with the desk clerk to see if they have cameras back here."

She just nodded and watched him get out of the vehicle. She turned and looked out the driver's side window. *Don't freak.*

She opened her car door and stepped out. Closing the door, she leaned against it. She peered into the side window of the SUV and saw Danny's phone in the console. Things were getting worse by the minute. He would never have left his phone behind. She went to the back of the SUV and picked up the suitcase hoisting it into the back alongside the other suitcase. She closed the trunk. She turned around and surveyed the area. Would Rayland have attacked Danny in broad daylight?

She went around to the driver's side and opened the door, getting inside. She sat behind the wheel and picked up his phone. It didn't have a password on it, so she was able to access it. She scrolled through his messages but didn't see anything concerning. She opened her own messages she had sent him, all unread.

She set the phone back down.

Danny, where are you?

The passenger side door opened, and Riley slid in. "They have no information, but they do have video. Come inside."

She stared at him; she wasn't sure that she wanted to see anything.

"C'mon, Harley."

She slipped out of the vehicle, pushing the door closed behind her. She followed Riley back through the front of the hotel and up to the front desk.

"Mr. Dawson, we have the tape available for viewing, if you'll follow me to the office in the back." A short, pudgy woman was standing behind the desk. Her hair coiffed into a perfect, sleek bob. It struck Harley how kind her eyes were.

"Of course. This is my partner, Harley Wolfhart."

Harley looked at him with a raised eyebrow and he smirked.

"Nice to meet you."

Harley smiled as they followed the woman behind the desk and into a brightly lit room in the back.

"We do record our parking lots daily all around the

hotel. We try to protect our customers as much as we can. It's mainly used in the case of theft or damage to property. They are only viewed the next day so we wouldn't have known that anything happened to your friend until tomorrow. We just don't have the time to watch the tapes all day."

"Understandable. If we can get any leads, it would be a great help."

She sat down at the desk and Harley and Riley circled behind her. She slid a tape into the tape deck and powered up the monitor. She fast-forwarded the tape until it was closer to the time that Danny checked out of their room.

Harley gasped. They watched as Danny left the hotel by the side door, near where the SUV was parked. He was pulling two suitcases as he walked to the SUV. He pulled out his keys, pressed a button and the trunk hatch slowly opened. As he was putting one suitcase into the back, a car drove slowly behind him and parked two cars down from the SUV.

"He's not paying attention."

Harley didn't need to see the rest of the video to know who was going to come out of the vehicle. What was shocking to her was that he wasn't alone.

"Oh my God."

Riley bent down closer to the screen. "Who is that?"

Harley swallowed hard. "Her name is Rebecca."

He snapped his head back at her. He looked back at the screen, and they watched as the pair casually walked over to Danny. He was too busy flinging the suitcases into the back of the car. He had forgotten everything he was trained for. He thought he was safe. He thought that there was only one target, and he couldn't have been more wrong.

Rayland was pulling something out of his pocket.

"Is that syringe?"

Harley was frozen in place, her throat closing up; she could barely breathe.

Danny must have seen movement out of the corner of his eye because his head started to turn towards it. But he was too late; the syringe was in his neck. He lashed out, trying to hit his attackers, but didn't make any contact. Harley wanted to scream into the screen and tell him to run. But she knew it wouldn't do him any good. Whatever was in that syringe was already taking effect as he started to stumble. As Danny was beginning to fade, both Rayland and Rebecca threw his arms over their shoulders. They walked him slowly to the car as if he were just a drunk friend who needed help getting home. Harley looked around the parking lot to see if there were any witnesses. Anyone that might have seen anything.

Rebecca opened the door to the backseat, and they pushed Danny inside, slamming the door behind him.

"Oh my god," the clerk whispered. "I just witnessed a kidnapping."

Harley couldn't believe her eyes when she saw the two killers smiling and giving each other high fives.

Rebecca walked around to the other side of the car and got into the passenger seat. Rayland paused, and she watched as he opened her SUV and reached inside, pulling something out.

"The files." She whispered.

She looked over at Riley, and he shook his head.

"What the fuck is going on here?" Confusion filled Harley like a fog. How long had those two been working together? It seemed as if they had known each other forever.

Riley looked at her. "I'm assuming there's a story here that I'm missing."

She looked at him, her eyes wide. "This nightmare just got exponentially worse."

Riley looked back at the screen. They watched as the car pulled away, driving out of view.

"Can you rewind that?" Harley asked.

The clerk rewound the video until the car was back in its spot.

"Can you zoom in?"

Harley watched as the license plate came into view.

"I'll call it in."

"He's too smart. He would have ditched the vehicle by now." Harley said.

"It's the only lead we have right now."

She nodded. He was right.

Riley looked at the clerk. "We're going to need to interview everyone of your guests. Someone might have seen something important."

The clerk looked stunned.

"I'm going to call in some backup to help us out. Harley, are you okay?"

She stared at the screen. *Danny, where are you?*

She turned quickly and left the room.

"Harley," he shouted.

"I have to make a phone call."

She walked around the desk and made her way to the front entrance of the hotel. Her stomach rolled, and she worried that she was going to be sick. She pulled out her phone and called the Sheriff in Georgia. She waited as the phone rang and then a voice on the other end.

"Harley? I'm surprised to hear from you. Is everything okay?"

"No, everything is not fucking okay."

There was silence, and then, "What happened?"

"How long have you known that the Butcher was connected to Rebecca?"

"What are you talking about?"

"I found her, Sheriff. She's with the Butcher."

He gasped. "No. That can't be."

"She is and I want to know what the connection is. You're telling me you really didn't know?"

"How could I? The Butcher hasn't even been out that long. Tell me what happened. How do you know they are together?"

"I found them on video together, outside of a hotel. They took Danny. They have him, together."

"Dear God. Harley, I'm so sorry. I had no idea, I swear. We have been working around the clock, searching for her. We assumed at this point that she jumped states. I guess we were right about that. She's gone."

"How? Can you think of anything that could tie them together? Were they friends and we just didn't know it?"

"No, there's no way. It's too much of a coincidence. The probability of them even being together is astronomical. Harley, didn't you say that he was following you? That he seemed to know where you were at all times?"

"Yes," she said hesitantly.

"Do you think that he found out why you were here and intercepted?"

The silence between them was deafening.

"No. Rebecca would just get into a car with that lunatic?"

"Well, if you think about it, they're two peas in a pod. Did you ever see the movie, *Natural Born Killers*?"

She chuckled. "Yes, the perfect killer couple. That makes me sick to my stomach."

"Actually, I find it pretty terrifying. He was lethal enough on his own. Now he has a partner."

"Well, she can hardly plead innocence now. If we get her, she won't have a leg to stand on with your case. How is the girl?"

"She's not speaking. I think she's scared that her mother will come back and finish the job. We're working on her, though; she's talking to a psychiatrist. We have a court order to keep the mother away from her if she happens to show up. She won't be talking to her daughter anytime soon. Now that she's been seen with the Butcher, we have enough to keep her away from the child. She and the therapist have an interesting relationship."

"In what way?"

"The psychiatrist asked her if she knew who shot her. She said yes but wouldn't tell her who. The doctor told her to write it on a piece of paper and then they would light it on fire. They do this at every meeting. The doctor said that when she was ready, they would open the paper together."

"That's incredible."

"Yeah, sad though, so far the papers have gone in the fire."

"Fear is a powerful thing. She'll come around, she's a strong girl. She made it through all of this."

"Oh, I forgot to tell you, we found something. I can't believe I haven't mentioned it by now."

"What?"

"Well, we had done an initial search of her place and found very little evidence to explain why she would do this but yesterday, I sent a crew in to do another search."

"What did you find?"

"We found something in the back of her kid's closet. We really weren't focusing on that area the first time. There was a statue, really weird. It looks more like something that would go on a gravestone. There was an inscription on it. It has the kid's names on it, and it says, 'I love you, mom,' and then the date of the shooting."

"You're kidding me."

"It looks as if she bought it for them as a gift. But we found the receipt, and it was purchased a week before the shooting. Like it's a memorial for the kids. Damn, I would love to have her here to question her about it."

"She's horrific. I can't wrap my head around someone who would do that to their children. And now it looks like it was pre-meditated. Giving that gift to her children is truly barbaric. So, you said that you thought you had a motive as to why she did it?"

"It's over a guy."

"No."

"Seems that way. She kept a journal and wrote about this guy that she was in love with. He was an old boyfriend from years ago, and she really never got over him. I think he was in love with her too, but there was just one problem."

She sighed. "He didn't want kids."

"Bingo. Judging by her entries, he broke things off with her because of that. She was devastated and was trying to find a way around it. There's nothing in the journals about wanting to harm her children, but the implication is there that she wished that she didn't have them so she could be with him."

"Interesting. Those poor kids. I can't imagine what they were going through knowing their mother did that to them. That image would be the last thing two of them saw."

"I know. Sometimes, no matter what you do, there's no justice in the world. Even throwing her in prison or giving her the death penalty isn't enough for what she did."

"You should prepare yourself for the possibility that she's not coming back alive."

"Why's that?"

"I don't know. The Butcher works alone. I don't know him to even want a partner."

"He wanted you, didn't he?"

She shuddered. "I guess. But apparently, he's still hung up on me." She laughed nervously.

"Maybe you'll get lucky, and he's falling for someone else."

"A girl can dream."

"I'm really sorry about Danny, Harley. It's a damn shame. I hope you find him."

"Me too." She said goodbye and ended the call.

TWELVE

HARLEY SAT AT THE BAR of Skipper's, a local dive bar, about ten minutes from Savannah's place. It wasn't very busy in the bar aside from a few regulars. The bartender got along well with them, joking easily and enquiring about their families.

"Ma'am, can I get you anything?"

"I'll have a Makers and Coke."

The bartender smiled and grabbed a rock glass, filling it with ice. She poured whiskey generously over the ice, at least a four-second pour. She took the fountain gun and added Coke to the glass, adding a short straw at the end. She placed the glass in front of her, and Harley slid over a twenty.

Harley pulled the straw from the glass and set it on the bar. She took a long drink from the glass and thought about the day. The entire day had been spent interviewing everyone at the hotel. The local sheriff's department had offered to help and sent over some guys to talk to guests. Sadly, for the hotel, some of those guests immediately checked out of the hotel. She couldn't really blame them. Even though it wasn't the hotel's fault, people wanted to feel safe. They questioned everyone and even called people who had already checked out. Not one person saw anything. The Butcher's timing was epic because there wasn't a soul who had any idea what had happened in that parking lot that day. It wasn't long before the news crews started showing up, and then it hit the stations. At least there was a video out there now of the pair. She could only hope that someone would recognize seeing them somewhere else. Too much time had passed, and she worried that they were too late. The Butcher never kept his victims for long. They had run the tags and put an APB out on the car, but so far, nothing had come up. All they could do now was wait, and so she decided she needed a drink.

She turned and looked at a grizzly-looking gentleman at the end of the bar, a grey labrador at his feet. She watched as he ordered two different beers, a Coors Light and a Bud Zero. The bartender brought him both, and he proceeded to pour the Bud Zero in the dog's bowl. She raised an eyebrow when the man made eye contact with her. He shrugged and said, "Guys night out."

She smiled even though she didn't feel like it. She turned back to her drink, staring into the glass. She gulped the whole thing and then ordered another.

It had only been three months since she had been on the island, but it still felt like it was yesterday. Her family had encouraged her to relax and take some time off before jumping into a business. But she couldn't do it. Her skin had prickled with nervous energy. She had nightmares for weeks after returning home. Every time that she did take a minute to relax, horrible images would crop up in her head. Her friends mutilated bodies, the room of severed heads, the graves in the mines. Her mind still couldn't process some of the things that she had seen. Her body wasn't even fully recovered from the trauma she endured on the island. She still couldn't go for a run without getting wounded from the collapsed lung. She couldn't just stay home and relax because if she tried even for a moment, she would be transported back to Thailand, where all the horrors began.

The horrors were back, and now she was losing her friends and coworkers again. She was going to be left alone with no one. That was what the Butcher wanted until she returned to him. She would rather be dead, and maybe that was what it was going to come down to. So many people had lost their lives because a man had become obsessed with her. What was she going to tell Danny's girlfriend if she didn't get him back?

The barking laughter of a regular broke through her thoughts as she looked down the bar. A biker in jeans and a t-shirt with a club vest on was easily in his 70's. He was laughing with his buddy, and the bartender was shaking her head.

"If you keep it up, Bobby, I'm going to have to cut you off."

"Naw, I got room for more of those two-dollar shots. You want to see my sperm whale tattoo?"

The girl shook her head as she poured him another.

"I got a story for you. My ex-wife didn't trust me much, and she made me get a tattoo above my package that said Jeannie's man."

Harley raised her eyebrows and looked at him incredulously. The elder's friend was roaring in his seat.

"Now, why would you go and do that, Bobby?"

"Oh, I didn't care. The problem was, she left me. So, my new wife wasn't a fan of the tattoo and said that she wasn't going to go down there as long as my ex's name was there. So, I covered it up with a sperm whale. Do you want to see it?"

"No one wants to see your sperm whale, Bobby. I doubt there's even a tattoo down there."

Harley started laughing as the rest of the bar roared around her.

"It's nice to see you smiling again."

She whipped her head around and looked into deep, striking blue eyes.

"God, why are you so handsome?"

Riley laughed. "I guess you can thank my mother for that." She sighed as he sat down beside her, motioning for the bartender.

"What can I get for you?"

"I'll have whatever she's having and bring her

another. She looks like she could use it."

"Shut up. What are you doing here?"

"Well, I was worried about you. This has been a rough day for everyone, but it's especially rough on you because you know the victim."

"Possible victim."

He stared at her. "Of course. They found his vehicle abandoned at a Chick-fil-A." The waitress brought their drinks, and Harley took a swallow.

"Now, the only thing we can do is wait for him to strike again. He's good at staying hidden. He won't make himself known until he wants to."

"I'm not worried. I know we have something that he wants."

Her eyes flicked to him.

"Sorry," he said with a shrug.

"Trust me. I would rather him just come and get it over with. I just don't want anyone else to die."

"You know it's not your fault."

"Yes, that's what my brain tells me, but my heart says something completely different. I could have left Danny at home."

"I bet he would have told you that it's his job. It's the business, he knew what he was getting into."

The bartender brought them another round of drinks. It wasn't getting any busier in the establishment.

"Is there someone waiting at home for you, Harley? Anyone worried about you?"

She stared into her drink. Picking it up, she drank

from the glass. It was good; despite the cola, it burned going down. It was a good pour. She was starting to feel a buzz coming along the edges.

"No, there's no one at home." She smiled at him. *He really was handsome.* His face was close and if she really wanted to, she could kiss him. But she didn't have it in her. Not anymore. Something had died inside her on the island and for the first time in her life, she was scared to feel anything for anyone.

"What is it, Harley?" He was staring at her in a way that made her heart flutter. She really needed to stop getting herself in these situations.

"The last time that I was intimate with a man, he turned out to be a notorious serial killer. That's not something you get over. Before that, I was in love with my partner, and he died." She smiled weakly. "There's a wall there now and I can't even imagine letting it down anytime soon."

He nodded before taking a sip of his drink.

"Harley, I get what you're saying, but you know just as much as I do that serial killers wear masks. You know this. The reason why they get away with so much is because they don't act or even look like serial killers. Rayland is a good-looking guy; he doesn't appear weird or creepy. He's charming, and that's how a lot of killers are. God, look at Ted Bundy. He even had girls swooning over him in the courtroom during his trial. They were obsessed with him because he was handsome and charismatic."

"Stop, Riley. I know. But it hits a little different when you're the one it happened to. Ted Bundy also had a girlfriend, and she was ostracized for her relationship with Bundy because no one wanted to believe that she really didn't know."

He leaned over and kissed her, making her body hum. She pulled away too soon and she watched his face fall.

"Kissing me is a good way to end up dead."

"He doesn't own you, Harley."

"He thinks that he does. You don't know what it's like to get close to someone, truly connect with them, and realize too late that there is a monster beneath the surface? I felt his soul, or I thought I did. I wanted to be with him; the connection was that strong. So, what does that say about me? I feel so stupid."

"Is that why you left the NYPD? Because you felt like you should have known."

"They talk about the cop instinct, don't they? But no, that wasn't the only reason. My partner turned out to be dirty; I was the one that put him down in the end. It made me lose faith in the entire system."

"Shit, I'm sorry. Trusting your partner is everything because they have your life in their hands."

"Yeah, he was my best friend and I had no idea."

"There's nothing wrong with your instincts. Rayland fooled everyone; the only person he didn't fool was his mother, and she got to see him discover himself from an early age. If you want to blame someone, blame her. Blame your partner and his weakness but stop blaming yourself."

"C'mon."

"No, Savannah knew who he was a very long time ago, and she chose to protect him instead of turning him in. So many lives could have been saved had she sought out help when he was young. If he couldn't be helped, he should have at least been hospitalized."

She finished her drink and signaled for another.

"I left the NYPD because I learned in Thailand that there were a whole lot of rules that prevented me from helping find the killer in the first place. I also learned from my old partner that you can't even trust the person that you're driving around with."

"Is being a private investigator the safe option for you?"

She laughed. "Hardly. After all, look where I am. But at least I get to play the game by my own rules and choose the cases that I believe in. Of course, no one wants to choose this case; I'm not even in charge of it."

He chuckled. "I'm not sure anyone is in charge of this one. We're all being taken for a ride."

"I think that you should have Savannah's property excavated."

Riley choked on his whiskey. "What the hell for?"

"She admitted to Danny and me that there was a teenager that Rayland dated when he was young. She went missing."

"Jesus."

"She believes that he killed her. She has no idea where the body is."

"She knew. That woman should be brought up on charges."

"It wouldn't hold up. You know that. But yeah, she knew. It would be nice to give that family some closure after all these years."

"You think he would be able to bury it in her backyard without her knowing?"

She sighed. "I think there's a lot that he did without her knowing."

"Alright, I'll call that in, but it won't be a priority."

Harley's phone rang, and she picked it up from the bar. She didn't recognize the caller. Her heart galloped around as she wondered if it was Rayland.

"Hello?"

"Harley? Is this Harley?"

"Yes, who is this?"

"It's Lucy, Danny's girlfriend." The girl started crying on the other end. "Danny is all over the news. He's on the news here in New York. What the hell is going on? Where's Danny?" She screamed.

Harley looked at Riley.

THIRTEEN

"IT CAN ONLY BENEFIT US that it's everywhere now. Maybe someone will see him, recognize him before the trail gets cold." Harley said.

The two agents and Harley were sitting at the kitchen table discussing yesterday's turn of events. Savannah had made them breakfast and then disappeared to another part of the house. She seemed to have relaxed since the agents arrived. Harley had talked the agents through the case going on in Georgia with the little girl who had been shot by her mother and the little boy who was now dead. She explained who the woman was in the video and how they had no idea how she ended up with the Butcher.

"Who the fuck leaked the video?" Agent Walter's barked.

She shrugged. "No idea. It could have been anyone at the hotel. We were there all day. One of those news vans probably paid off the right person."

"All it's going to do is start a panic."

"Good."

He glared at Harley. "I'm getting really sick of you. You're lucky you're not on the force because I would have sent you home a long time ago."

"For what? Cause you don't like me?"

"You're too close to this. People who know you are dying. You can't stay neutral any longer."

"Well, I guess it's a good thing that you can't send me home."

He smirked. "Do you really believe that just because you're a P.I., I can't get rid of you? I work for the Bureau, sweetheart. There's plenty I could do."

She walked right into his face. "Do it. I don't care. If you think for a moment that I enjoy being in the lion's den, you're kidding yourself. But let's be honest, you wouldn't have a first clue about what he was doing if I wasn't here. You certainly didn't help protect Danny. I would be better off going back to Georgia to help the sheriff's department with their case."

They glared at each other before Riley came between them.

"Let's try to remember, guys, that we're on the same team. Sheldon knows that you're an asset here. He's just being a dick."

"What?"

"You know you are. If Harley left here, Rayland would just follow her, and we would be twiddling our thumbs here for no reason. Everything that Rayland has done so far has been connected to Harley. For fuck sakes, he even went and got a new girlfriend from a case that Harley advised on. The best thing that we could do at this point is to try to figure out what connection to Harley he's going to go after next."

They all fell silent because none of them had any idea what the Butcher's next move was going to be. He had surprised them every step of the way.

"I mean, aside from trying to clean up loose ends, his actions imply that he's trying to hurt me. I don't think there's anyone left for him to take. Any survivors from the island are gone, and my partner is gone."

"No boyfriends?" Sheldon said with a sneer.

"None. Now any man that Rayland's might feel threatened by is up for grabs. I think that's why he grabbed Danny. If he even thinks that I might be involved with another man, that person's life is in danger."

"What about family?"

"I don't have any. My mother is still alive, but I haven't seen her in years. She's an addict. If she's even still alive, I would have no idea where she was. He's taken everyone else away from me."

Harley turned around to find Savannah hovering in the doorway of the kitchen. "Everything okay, Savannah?"

"Yes. All of this is just making me a bit jumpy. Not knowing where he is."

Savannah had not heard from Rayland at all, and Harley was even surprised that he had not called her to gloat about Danny. Maybe that meant that Danny was still alive somewhere. She could only hope. She thought about the call that came from his girlfriend, Lucy. She had sounded so scared on the other line and Harley had been unable to offer her any hope. Maybe she should have called her to warn her, but she hadn't expected it to go nationwide. She was still holding out hope that Danny was going to be okay, and she didn't want to worry her. Really, the truth was, she hadn't even thought about her. Things were so crazy that she had forgotten that Danny had someone back home waiting for him to return.

This is all your fault! That was the last thing that Lucy had said to her before she had hung up on her. She was probably right. It had been Harley's choice to bring him with her. She could easily have sent him to Georgia and went to Savannah's on her own. But like Riley had already said, it was his job, and he knew that the Butcher was loose at the time. He knew the risks. But that didn't make her feel any less guilty about it. She knew the only reason the Butcher went after Danny was because of her. He wasn't worried about Danny being a physical threat; he just didn't want him anywhere around Harley. She could only pray that she would be able to bring Danny home safely to Lucy.

"Why hasn't he called?"

Harley narrowed her eyes. "Who?"

"Rayland."

"Why would he be calling you?"

"Well, he wouldn't... I mean." She stumbled over her words. "He has called before, and at least then I had some idea of where he was. He's been quiet for too long."

Harley stared at her, and her stomach turned. She was starting to think that she should have stayed at the hotel. Savannah wasn't acting like herself, and it was starting to creep Harley out.

FOURTEEN

"**WE MUST MAKE A SMALL** trip, my darling, and then we can go and see your daughter."

Rebecca groaned as she stood in front of the bathroom mirror. They had booked another Airbnb in a neighbouring town to get some rest. Rebecca was drying her hair in the bathroom after having a shower. It was easy for them to find places to stay because you could book an Airbnb online without ever seeing the person who owned it. Rebecca's name wasn't well known enough in New Orleans for there to be any red flags when she booked rooms. Rayland had all the money in the world to pay for anything that they needed. He heard the blow dryer turn on as she got ready for the day. It gave Rayland the time that he needed to put his plan into action. He had one more cut that he wanted to make into Harley's psyche before he made his way towards her. By the time he was done with her, she would be begging him to kill her.

Rebecca walked out of the bathroom, and Rayland smiled. "You look perfect."

She touched her newly dyed copper-red hair with her fingertips, fiddling with it. "Really, you like it?"

"Love it."

She looked uncertain. "I've always been a blonde."

"You look radiant. It's probably best to be unrecognizable right now. Plus, I love redheads."

She giggled, and he kissed her hard on the mouth.

"I don't understand why we have to go after Harley. Fuck her. Let's go get Cindy and then go to Spain together. We can start over."

He stared at her. He put his hand around her throat and squeezed. She looked up at him and gasped. Then she smiled, and he smiled down at her. "I told you that I have work to do. It's important work. I would not be able to enjoy Spain with you if I just allowed Harley to win."

"Are you in love with her like that guy said?"

Rayland froze. "No, my darling. He doesn't know anything. I need to end Harley. She put me in prison… in Singapore. I won't stop until I've killed her and everyone she knows. Then we can go off together."

She nodded.

"Now get your things packed because I have us booked on a redeye to New York."

"New York?"

FIFTEEN

THE WALLS OF THE CABIN were painted red. Harley had never seen so much blood. She walked inside in a daze, and she couldn't hear a thing. It was like she was inside a bubble, without any outside contact. There was a slight buzzing in her ears as she looked around the room.

What am I doing here?

She had fought to be at the crime scene. But once she was there, she would have paid any amount of money to be anywhere else. Despite the plastic that had been laid lovingly all over the floor, the room was wall-to-wall streaks of blood. She thought that she had walked into a *Nightmare on Elm Street* movie. The smell of the room was unbearable. The metallic scent of blood was all-consuming, sticking inside her nostrils. But that wasn't the worst of it. The smell of feces filled the room when Danny's bowels loosened upon his death. The most horrific death she had ever seen. She didn't think that Jigsaw could have performed better than the Butcher did.

"Harley. Harley. Harley!"

Railey was in her face. She blinked. Once, twice, she wasn't registering that Riley was talking to her.

"Harley, please. Harley."

He tried to pull her away, but she was staring into the middle of the room, where Danny was slumped in his chair.

The room came into focus, and she could suddenly hear everything going on in the room. There were cops everywhere as well as the FBI. The poor homeowners were on the front porch and the wife was sobbing hysterically. They would have to burn down the home or turn it into a horror museum because there wasn't another person on the planet that would rent the cabin out after news hit that the Butcher had paid a visit.

"Harley, are you okay?"

"How bad is it?"

"It's the worst I've ever seen. I have veteran officers losing their lunch in the backyard. I think you should wait outside."

"No, I have to see what happened. I'm responsible for Danny."

"No, Harley, you're not."

She walked past him and into the middle of the living room where Danny sat. Or what was left of him? It was no longer Danny who sat in the seat; he was unrecognizable, just like a pound of flesh sitting in the chair. They had mutilated him to the point where you couldn't even tell which body part was which. His left leg had been completely severed and found in the bathtub. The middle of his stomach was wide open, and she could see part of his ribcage, his intestines spilled on the floor in front of him. There was so much blood that it was pooled past the plastic and into the carpet. Her eyes trailed from the blood on the floor, all the way past his torso to his severed neck. There was no head. By now, tears were streaming down her face.

"Oh, Danny," she whispered.

"I'm sorry, Harley."

She turned her head to look at Riley, who was holding a handkerchief to his nose.

"Where is the head? Did he take it with him?"

"No. I don't think that he's interested in keeping souvenirs this time around. It seems like he just wants to send a message. A message to you, Harley."

"Where is the head," she whimpered.

"It's on the bed in the master bedroom, surrounded by all the files that he stole from your SUV. They're garbage, of course; they're covered in blood. Useless. And before you think of asking, no, you can't go in there. That's where I draw the line."

She simply nodded. She had seen enough. She had seen enough to keep her up at night for the rest of her life. Her stomach rolled, and she clutched at it. She tasted bile as it rose up in her throat. She bolted through the living room and out the back patio door. She sprawled out on the soft, green grass of the backyard as she emptied the entire contents of her stomach. She vomited until her throat was raw, and then she collapsed on her side in the grass. She stared up into the sky and watched as the clouds slowly drifted past. Danny was gone; that was official now. There was no getting around it. Any hope she had was dead, and now she would have to make a call to Lucy and tell her the type of news that would change her life forever.

Tears welled up in her eyes and then spilled down her cheeks like small rivers that would never dry up. They would constantly flow until there was nothing left inside of her. Maybe it was time for her to go home. If it was the Butcher's goal to break her, she was getting close to the edge. This was like no other case that she had experienced before. The Butcher was like no other killer she had heard of. He would go down in infamy over what he was doing, and that was if they ever caught him. How was he moving around undetected? How was he getting around? He must have had cash stashed somewhere, maybe even ID. That's why he was able to stay hidden, and now he had someone else with him to help him. She wondered if Rebecca had anything to do with the macabre mess that was in the living room.

Suddenly, Riley was above her, blocking her view of the clouds.

"You're killing my vibe."

He looked up into the sky and then back at her. "Sorry

about that. Looks like you joined the other officers."

She sat up and noticed two officers for the first time sitting at a patio table, one with his head in his hands. The other looked both pale and green. She didn't feel much better after emptying her stomach, and now she had a headache.

"Are you okay?"

"You sure like to ask me that a lot."

"Well, it's been a hell of a week. I can't blame you for getting sick; it's quite the scene in there."

She couldn't even think about the scene; it was so gruesome, and it was a million times worse because she knew the victim.

"I need to call his girlfriend."

"Let me do you a favor, and I'll do it. I think you have a lot on your plate already, and we're not even finished."

"I should be the one to call her."

"Harley, let me help you. It's perfectly fine if the agent in charge of the case calls her. They weren't married, so his belongings will go back to his parents."

"Okay. Fair enough." She squinted up at him. "Can you help me up?"

He smiled. He grabbed her outreached hand and pulled her up. "One thing that I can't figure out is why the Butcher even used plastic if he was going to leave such a mess. He's always been meticulous with hiding the evidence."

She nodded. "Yeah, well, I guess he has no reason to

hide anything. We all know who is murdering these people. As far as the plastic goes, I think he lost control."

"Lost control? That doesn't sound like the Butcher."

"Maybe that's not the right word. The reality is, I don't think that Rayland killed Danny."

Riley's eyes widened.

"That scene in there is not his M.O. He might be a butcher, but that was a blood bath. When I found his room of heads, they were completely devoid of mess, zero blood. He was that careful. We didn't know how he did it. And sure, maybe he doesn't care about us knowing who did the murder, but I don't think that is the answer. I think it's Rebecca. They're either sharing in the joy of murder together, or he found himself an apprentice. But either way, she did what we see in that room. I would bet money on it."

"Shit, you're right. This is insanity. We're basically hunting two killers down."

"Maybe we should bring in the Georgia PD," she said with a chuckle.

"The bureau is going to have to start contacting all the PDs in the area because it's pretty obvious that the main reason we can't get a handle on this is because the Butcher is constantly moving. He doesn't stay in one place for too long. Really, it's probably how he always stayed undetected before he met you. He loves to travel."

"Did Danny die right away? Was it quick?"

He looked down at the ground before meeting her

eyes again. "No. No he didn't."

She steeled herself so that the tears wouldn't spill from her cheeks. He pulled her in for a hug and she accepted it. She sobbed silently in his arms until she didn't have anything left. She was worn out. They parted and she looked into his eyes.

"I'm heading back to Savannah's house. I think I need to lay down."

"Understandable. We have all the manpower that we need right now. Go get some rest and we'll debrief when we get back."

"I'm surprised Savannah allowed everyone to be gone."

"To be honest, I think she was relieved to have some privacy for once."

"Yeah, she's a strange woman."

He walked her around the outside of the house until they got to the driveway. "Just take my car. I'll get a ride back with Sheldon."

She smiled. "I appreciate everything that you've done."

"Try to get some rest. This is only the beginning."

She turned and left him there with Danny. She didn't envy any of the crew that had to work there tonight. Most of them would probably never sleep soundly again. She slid into Riley's black SUV, started the engine and rolled away from that nightmare.

SIXTEEN

HARLEY STOOD IN THE BATHROOM, staring at herself in the mirror. She wasn't just staring; she was analyzing every inch of herself, from her vibrant red hair to her piercing blue eyes. She took a deep breath and looked down at the pee stick that was sitting on the bathroom sink. Her three minutes were up. She couldn't hide the truth anymore. She was pregnant.

She was pregnant with the Butcher's child.

SEVENTEEN

TWO DAYS HAD GONE BY without a word from the Butcher. Harley was walking around in a daze unable to hold any real conversations or focus on tasks at hand. They didn't have any leads and Savannah had taken up chain smoking. She couldn't figure out why she hadn't heard from Rayland. Harley was just hoping he got hit by a bus somewhere and they would never hear from him again. She wouldn't be that lucky, however.

She hadn't told anyone that she was pregnant. She couldn't even begin to understand how she would even have that conversation with anyone. She had a strong urge to throw herself down the stairs because the thought of what could be growing inside of her terrified her more than anything. Was being a psychopath hereditary?

She had never planned on having children, her own childhood had been enough of a nightmare to ensure she was always on birth control. She had never really thought about whether she would have children of her own. She figured that when she was with someone that she loved enough, they would figure it out together. But she was fully comfortable with never having children.

She sat at the writing desk that Savannah had in her living room. She was starting to think that she should get a hotel room again. It was looking like Savannah might not need further protection after all. They had discussed the possibility that the Butcher had killed Danny and then left the country again. He had the funds and means to travel so he could have easily slipped through their fingers. There were agents posted at the nearest airports to them, but Rayland had already proven that if he drove far enough away, he could slip away undetected.

There was a burst of activity outside, and she lifted herself up slightly to look out the window. There was a crime scene van and a digger out front. There were also another two agents in the front yard. Savannah was having a meltdown, screaming at Riley. The FBI had decided that since they had some downtime, they were going to look for a body. Harley's heart beat hard, and they thought that they might actually find something. Could there be a graveyard in Savannah's backyard? She shivered.

The front door slammed, and suddenly, Savannah appeared in the doorway of the living room. "This is your fault," she said through clenched teeth. She was seething, her whole body practically humming before Harley.

"Excuse me?"

"Those men out there are planning on digging up my backyard. What did you tell them?"

Harley shook her head slightly. "I would like to think you would want to know if there is a dead girl in your backyard, Savannah. It's not exactly good karma."

"There is nothing in my backyard."

"Then I will gladly apologize to you."

Savannah's hand went to her heart. Always the delicate flower. "You will pay for this, I promise you." She said as she spun around and left the room. Harley furrowed her brow. That was a side of Savannah that she hadn't seen before. She could hear the woman screeching in the backyard. Harley couldn't blame her for being upset. If word got out that she had bodies in her backyard, she might have to consider moving because she would be ostracized. Harley was surprised that her yard hadn't been searched much earlier. Everyone knew that Rayland grew up there and did some unspeakable things to animals. As far as she was concerned, the whole property should be searched. She sat back down at the desk, searching reconsidering staying at the house any longer. She couldn't stay there forever, and no one knew when and if Rayland was ever coming back.

She opened her laptop and started doing searches. The moment that Harley found out that she was pregnant, it was all that she could think about. All her moments of sickness all came into focus. She didn't have a weak stomach; she was just carrying a serial killer's baby in her womb. It was enough to upset anyone. She had been so stressed and preoccupied over the past couple of months that she hadn't realized that she missed her period. There had even been times over the years that stress had caused her to miss a period here and there. It had never once occurred to her that she could have gotten pregnant on the island. There was a slim possibility that the baby could also be Craig's, but that would add at least another week to the timeline, and that made it even more unlikely. *Ugh, she felt like such a hoe.*

That brought a smile to her face. She focused on the computer screen, feeling silly about her searches, but she was trying to find some comfort in the situation.

ARE PSYCOPATHS BORN OR MADE?

She stared at the over 2 million searches that popped up.

"Overall, and consistent with the findings culled from twin-based research, the results of these adoption-based studies have provided additional evidence that psychopathy, psychopathic personality traits, and other measures of psychopathology are influenced by genetic factors."

Not comforting. The consensus seemed to be that although psychopaths weren't born that way, the environment in which a child was raised could affect the child. Experts believed that there were some children born at high risk for developing psychopathy due to inherited genetic factors.

There was a lot of debate in the world about whether serial killers and psychopaths were born evil or if they learn the behavior. Rayland wasn't born in an abusive household, though he did have an absent father in his life. Harley knew Rayland and had often wondered what made him the way that he was. Despite what the experts said, Harley believed he was evil to the core. There wasn't anything human about a man who dismembered humans while they were still alive. There was no explaining that behavior. He was sick and there was no cure. He needed to be hospitalized or put down. So, what did that mean for the little human growing inside of her. She couldn't imagine keeping a child that was the Butcher's, but that wasn't the type of decision that should be taken lightly either. Tears welled up in her eyes. How the hell did she get herself into this mess? *His baby?* The very thought of it terrified her.

Riley walked in the room, and she quickly shut her laptop.

"Geez, Savannah is a spitting viper out there."

"If you find something, are we going to have to move?"

He shook his head. "No. We would have the remains removed and then tent off the whole area. But this place is our only connection to the Butcher, we can't take the chance of losing him by moving locations."

"Why? Because you're using me as bait?" She said nervously.

"You and Savannah are the only ones that have heard from him. This place is important. Savannah doesn't even have a cellphone."

Harley laughed.

"Normally, we would leave, but we have to stay even just for a little while longer until we know where he is. He's got to turn up at some point."

"I hope so. This waiting is starting to get to me."

"We got something!" There was a shout from outside, and Harley froze. A chill slinked its way up her spine and back down again.

"Oh my God."

"Let's go."

They hurried outside. There was a large white tent set up, covering the area where the crime scene techs were working. It allowed the area to be undisturbed by weather and offered maximum privacy against nosy neighbours. The yard was fenced but the fence wasn't high enough to completely block the situation from the neighbors. When they got outside, there were agents holding Savannah back, who was wailing near the back door. Her home was about to become a crime scene and Harley had to wonder whether there would be a For Sale sign placed in the front lawn in the future.

Two men were bent down in a hole, shovels in hand. She walked over slowly, unsure that she wanted to see anymore bodies.

"What did you guys find?" Riley barked. Sheldon moved into the scene from the back and stood at the edge of the hole, silent.

"We have a skeleton; it's in pretty good condition but not attached. Skull, torso and femur…" The crime scene tech started naming off the parts of the skeleton, and Harley's vision blurred.

"Is it her?" She asked.

"Too soon to tell. A lot of years have passed. We'll have to test the DNA and go from there. We're going to collect the specimen and bring it in now. Hopefully, they'll be able to give us an answer soon. We've combed the area. This seems like the only body here, thank God."

Harley turned to Riley. "Could you imagine if it's her?"

"They should be able to come up with a cause of death. At the very least, the parents will know what happened to her and can get some form of peace from that. It's the best that we can do."

"I can't imagine what her parents have gone through all this time. The wondering would be the worst. Never knowing what happened to her."

"It makes you wonder if they ever had any suspicions. I mean, usually, the boyfriends are the first suspects. I looked at her file."

"Did you? Oh my god, can I see it?"

"Yeah, I have it in the guest room. Rayland was never even questioned in her disappearance. So, it begs to question, who really knew that they were together? Was it just Savannah?"

"She did mention that she wasn't sure it was public knowledge. They spent a lot of time together, according to her, but whether they were actually "boyfriend/girlfriend" isn't known."

"I find it odd either way that he wasn't interviewed. If they spent any time together, he should have been. Someone dropped the ball."

"Savannah holds a lot of guilt inside for these things. I think she regrets staying silent."

He sighed. "If she does, it's because she's realizing that her life is just as much in danger as yours."

"You don't think she feels bad for not telling on him?"

"I don't know. She's a weird gal, but I don't get a whole lot of emotions from her. She's closed off. She should be hysterical at this point or guilt-stricken. But all I see is fear and worry for Rayland. I don't like her."

She wasn't exactly Harley's favorite person, but she felt sorry for her. She always had. She carried a huge burden her entire life and was never able to have a life of her own because of it. That would be punishment alone.

Harley watched as they delicately lifted out the remains and put them in black body bags. Anything too small went into small evidence bags.

"When will you contact the parents?"

"Only if the DNA comes back that it's her. We don't even know if the parents are still alive."

Harley turned to look at Savannah, who was clutching

a handkerchief and sobbing. She seemed more upset than shocked. Like a secret had been discovered that should have stayed buried. Harley didn't think that she would ever be able to understand her.

"C'mon, let's get a drink, and I'll show you the file."

She followed him inside, and she went to the fridge to grab them a couple of beers. By the time she reached the living room, he had returned from the guest room. Riley had the guest room, while Sheldon had a cot set up in the sewing room. The home had four bedrooms, and after Rayland left, she converted one into a sewing room, and the other two bedrooms were guest rooms. Harley was in the other guest room. She hoped that by some sick twist of fate, she wasn't actually occupying Rayland's old room. It was a true testament to the determination of the FBI to snatch Rayland at that location because she still couldn't believe that Sheldon had agreed to sleep on a cot.

He handed her the shockingly thin file, and she opened it up. It was very old, pre-digital era when things were either handwritten or typed with a typewriter. Neighbors, friends, and family had been interviewed, but not Rayland or Savannah. There was no mention of the young girl having a boyfriend in the file. Maybe the whole thing was unknown. It would have made it easier for Rayland to get away with killing her.

The parents were Tanya and Glen Parks. She looked over at Riley. "Oh my god, how do you kill a girl named Daisy?"

"The interview with the parents is the worst. Parents always go overboard with their kids, and in my job anyways, I often wonder if they make half of it up to make their kid seems perfect. But this one might actually have been. Straight A student, never in trouble, never missed a curfew. Just the sweetest thing, according to her parents. How she ever got wrapped up with Rayland is beyond me. We interviewed the teachers though from the school a while back when Rayland was first caught, and he was seen as a handsome young man, shy, but I don't think anyone worried about their daughter dating him. Which was a little different from when he was a kid, and the neighborhood pets would go missing."

Sheldon walked in the room. "I could use a beer. Thanks for the invite. Savannah is foaming at the mouth out there, so I wouldn't be surprised if she kicks us out tonight. Good job, though, Harley with suggesting we drag the backyard."

She was surprised that he threw a compliment her way, but she wasn't about to complain. She simply nodded.

"You're the devil! I should have known right from the beginning."

Harley's mouth dropped open as Savannah came in the room behind Sheldon.

"What the hell?" Riley said. Sheldon started turning around, but Savannah passed him as she came further into the room. She was holding something in her hand, and the hairs on Harley's arms prickled.

"You have a demon inside you."

"Oh shit," she whispered.

She could see what Savannah was holding now. The pregnancy test that she threw in the bathroom trash can. She had found it. *God, why couldn't she be better at this?*

"Savannah, have you lost your damn mind?" Sheldon was hollering now.

Riley saw what was in her hand and glanced at Harley, confused. Then understanding came over his face, and his eyes widened.

"You're pregnant," he said, almost a whisper.

"Yes," Harley choked out.

Savannah swayed and then dropped like a stone at Harley's feet. Harley dropped down beside her and checked her vitals. "Riley, grab a cold cloth."

She looked up at Sheldon, who was shaking his head. "Forget what I said earlier; you're a hot mess."

Harley rubbed her face and finally dragged her hands through her hair.

Well, she couldn't argue with him there.

EIGHTEEN

THE STENCH OF NEW YORK ALWAYS bothered the Butcher. He couldn't imagine why anyone would want to live in such a dirty city. The only signs of life were in Central Park, and even that was man-made. But somehow, the celebrities and the elites moved to the Upper East Side in flocks, forgetting that there was a large part of New York run by rats, both figuratively and literally. That was where Harley chose to live. He didn't know how to feel about the fact that she left the NYPD and decided to go off on her own. Even though New York was her home, it was also the last place that they would be looking for him. He wore a ballcap and sunglasses and had shaved off the beard that was part of the photo that was being circulated of him. He could only do so much to disguise himself, aside from keeping his head down. He didn't plan on being in any high-traffic areas. He knew what he was looking for; he planned on getting in and getting out.

Rebecca turned out to be a breath of fresh air. The more that she was around, the more that he enjoyed not being alone so much. That was the type of life that he had wanted with Harley, but she had turned her back on him and was now working with the enemy. He had tried multiple times to convince her to join him, to rule the world alongside of him. But she had rejected him, and she would pay for that.

Rebecca was a willing apprentice with a strong stomach. He was proud of the work that she did with Danny. Albeit messy, she did good work. He would have to teach her to work a crime scene so that she could do her work without the mess or worry that she was leaving too much evidence behind. Evidence didn't matter now; everyone knew who was leaving bodies in their wake. That allowed them freedom to do what they wanted to and move on to the next victim. He tried to imagine what it was like for Harley to go in there and see her boy toy a heap of flesh. Her terror and her revulsion fueled him and made him feel alive. He would make her feel as much pain as possible before he snuffed out her life, and he was only getting started. During the trip, Rebecca had been calling every homeless shelter in the main vicinity of where Harley lived. He knew a little about Harley's mother from the confessions she had made on the island. Rebecca impersonated Harley and asked for any information about her mother. People were willing to bend over backward for the famous NYPD officer who helped bring down a serial killer. He bristled. They got lucky when they got a hit at a local shelter not three blocks from Harley's old apartment. Her name was Mandy, and she rarely stayed at the shelter, but the residents knew a place where she liked to hang out. He sent Rebecca on an errand and went to grab a coffee at a stand on the corner of the street. He accepted the hot coffee gratefully and sat on a street bench as he waited for Rebecca to bring him the goods. This was going to be the easiest abduction that he had ever done, but possibly the most satisfying.

He sipped the coffee and smelled the sweet air coming from the sewers. He couldn't wait to get out of the city. He had one more task after he left New York before he would return for Harley. Everything was falling into place perfectly. He had no reason to believe that he wouldn't succeed.

Rebecca plopped on the bench beside him. She was smirking.

"Did you get it?"

She bit her lip and nodded. He smiled.

"Okay, let's go hunting."

The sun was starting to set before the Butcher came across the woman that spawned Harley. One of the most common places that Mandy used to go was in the tunnels under the Grand Central Station. Going into those tunnels was not for the meek. But the Butcher didn't worry about who he would meet up. He was most people's worst nightmare; he didn't fear anyone else. There was a folklore of the "mole people" that lived within the tunnel. Made of cement, it was often wet and dingy in the tunnels, but the area was still lit with lightning on the roof of the tunnels. But there were plenty of shadows in between each light. The two walked along the edge of the tunnel, and there was an area up ahead where a group of vagrants were trying to get warm over a bucket of fire. They were in trench coats and fingerless gloves, rubbing their hands vigorously together.

It wasn't hard to find Mandy because she had the same vibrant red hair that Harley had. She was aged beyond her years due to life on the streets and drug abuse, but she still didn't have one grey hair on that brilliant redhead. She was a frail, stick of a woman in baggy clothes. The Butcher looked at Rebecca.

"This will be your next assignment, darling."

She smiled. She was enjoying the process just as much as he was. There was a hard belief that women weren't natural killers, but that couldn't be further from the truth.

He sent Rebecca over to talk to the woman because she was less threatening-looking than he was. They had purchased some 'mollys' and some GHB on the street as a means of luring the woman away. An addict wouldn't be able to resist the temptation of free drugs.

The Butcher moved into the shadows and watched as Rebecca approached her. The two women talked for a few moments. At first, Mandy was shaking her head, not wanting to leave the fire pit. Then Rebecca dug around in her pocket and pulled out the drugs. Mandy looked around and grabbed Rebecca's arm, pulling her away from the other people before they could see what she had. The two whispered amongst each other, their heads close together. Rebecca was pointing in the direction of where the Butcher was standing. He smiled as he watched the two women approach. Mandy was startled as he came out of the shadows and drew a wary eye towards Rebecca, who assured her everything was fine.

"Hello, Mandy, I'm a friend of Harleys', it's nice to meet you."

A sour look came over her face. "That girl gave me nothing but trouble. I haven't even seen her in years."

He nodded, a headache coming on. "Come then, we have much to discuss."

Cutting into flesh released something in the Butcher. He would get terrible headaches in between kills. Being in prison had almost been the end of him. He needed to kill; it was a part of him. The headaches were debilitating, and the best that he could do in prison was break someone's nose and watch them bleed.

There was something about watching that river of blood flow when he made that first cut. It was like taking pain reliever medication. The headache just instantly went away. That cut, that slice, the tear from a saw, the hole that the drill made, it was all music to him, and the sight of blood thrilled him. He couldn't go for long without another kill. He was always looking for the next victim.

The shock that came over Mandy's face when he started to tear into her skin was truly astounding. What did she think was going to happen when she willingly let them tie her to a chair? Anything for a fix, and they gave her exactly what she wanted. More than enough drugs to stone her out, but not to avoid the pain. The kind of pain that he planned on bestowing to her couldn't be masked with any type of drug. He closed his eyes and listened as the vibration of *The Four Seasons* by Vivaldi reverberated from Rebecca's phone. He cut into her femur but made sure to avoid any arteries. He wanted her to bleed but not to bleed out. He felt a stir in his loins as the blood pooled out and dripped off her body. He could feel Rebecca chomping at the bit as she awaited her turn. She was exquisite when she worked, and he couldn't wait to make love to her when they were finished. The both covered in their victim's blood. They had rented another Airbnb, a small house in a quiet neighbourhood. Mandy had walked willingly into the home, so he didn't worry much about what the neighbors might think. It was different that time as he had Rebecca go into the local Target and purchase a small video camera. He wanted it all recorded and remembered. He couldn't do it on her phone because then he wouldn't have his music, and that was essential.

Mandy was screaming now against the gag in her mouth. He smiled at her. "You can thank your daughter, Harley, for this."

Tears rolled down the woman's face as she continued to scream.

The Butcher looked back at Rebecca and motioned for her to grab a tool on the table. She picked up a hand saw that she purchased from Home Depot and brought it over.

"You need to think about your work, my love and take pride in it. Let's try not to make the same kind of mess that we made last time."

She blushed as if she had made some small faux pas that could be waved away.

Mandy passed out the moment that Rebecca began to saw off her arm.

Cleaning up was a lot easier that time because the Butcher was able to rein Rebecca's thirst in a little more. She liked a good bloodbath; the spray of blood against the wall or the pool of it beneath the chair. He cleaned off the tools before putting them away in a satchel that he purchased. The rest of the drugs were still on the table, and he just left them there. He liked to carry his own tools, he always had. He would have to replace them again in Spain, but he was okay with that. He turned back to Mandy, who slumped in the chair; she no longer had a head, and they had removed her spine.

Rebecca approached him.

"It's time to go and get Cindy."

He nodded. "The video was recorded properly?"

"Yes." She handed him her phone. He wondered if he had enough time to watch it again.

He looked at her, smiling up at him, her face splattered with blood. He leaned in and kicked her passionately, their tongues finding each other. He grasped her hand and moved her towards the bedroom. They started removing their clothes before they could even get the bedroom door closed.

Before they left the Airbnb, the Butcher looked up the email address for Harley's business and sent the video they created to her from Rebecca's phone. He smiled when he pressed sent, hoping that would be the thing that finally broke her.

They had another flight booked to go to Georgia and he felt thrilled to see Rebecca's daughter. He knew that there would probably be security there, but he was confident that he could get passed them. It wouldn't be the first time that he moved through the shadows to get what he wanted. If Rebecca wanted to visit her daughter, then he would make sure that it happened. She had proved to be a worthy partner and he would give her what she wanted. He looked around the living room, just as they had left it; there was no need to cleanup any longer. He was proud of the work that they did together. She needed more training in keeping the crime scene clean, but he was sure that she would get better at it with practice.

"It's almost over and then we can leave and start a whole new life together."

She smiled a chilling smile, not an ounce of warmth to it. He felt himself grow aroused.

"Maybe we have a few more minutes before we leave."

NINETEEN

HARLEY WAS ALONE IN THE HOUSE. She sat on the front porch, drinking a cup of tea. It was a nice neighborhood, perfect for raising a family. There were no sounds of the city or sirens in the distance. Just children laughing in the distance or a dog barking. Savannah had a few appointments to attend to and wanted to stop at the grocery store. No one had heard from Rayland in a while, so they felt safe to allow her to go on her own.

Riley and Sheldon were at a meeting in the city. It was being determined if they had lost a handle on the case and whether their efforts were needed somewhere else. She was also starting to wonder if she should return to New York. They were all starting to get on each other's nerves at that point. Everyone's nerves were frayed trying to figure out why Rayland had stopped making contact. They needed to regroup and figure out if the investigation needed to go in another direction. She had to call Roxie and tell her about Danny, and her poor assistant had sat on the phone with her crying. Losing Danny was a huge loss for everyone. Roxie was terrified for Harley and wanted her to come home. The last thing that Harley wanted was for Roxie to be in danger, so she called the Captain and asked him to put a squad car on her. Roxie had filled her in on the new hires who were clearing up the overload of cases quite well.

She noticed a woman watching her from the sidewalk. She stared at her until the woman got the courage to walk up the sidewalk and onto the porch.

"Savannah isn't home."

"That's good to know."

Harley smiled. "Can I help you?"

"There's been a lot of rumors going on in the neighborhood. People talking about the digging going on in Savannah's backyard."

"I can't really go into that right now. It's a police matter."

The woman cringed. "We were all hoping she would have moved away a long time ago. There's something wrong with that family. When it came out what her awful boy did on that island, we were all beside ourselves. And still, she didn't move. Now you're all digging in her background. I'm about ready to put my house up for sale."

"I understand how you must feel, but I'm not at liberty to discuss this right now. You'll likely hear about it in the next few days, but for now, there are certain people who could get hurt by leaked information."

"Oh dear." The woman clutched her chest.

"If I could offer any advice to you, it is to keep your doors locked and get a security system if you don't already have one."

The woman paled visibly, nodded, and then headed off the porch without another word. It was at that moment that Savannah's Buick pulled into the driveway.

Savannah left her groceries in the car and hurried up the pathway to the porch.

"What was Mildred doing here?"

"She was curious about the digging in the backyard."

Savannah looked like she might pass out. "What did you say to her?"

"I was clear that I couldn't talk about it. I'm not about to sit here gossiping with the neighbors about a police investigation."

"The more I get to know you, Harley, the less I like you. I think you're up to something?"

"The way you behaved yesterday didn't impress me much either, Savannah. You made my being pregnant public knowledge. You could have taken me aside and talked to me about it. The FBI certainly didn't need to know at this stage of the game."

She looked at Harley with thinly veiled disgust, and it shocked her. Something had changed in Savannah, and Harley couldn't put her finger on it. What had changed in the past couple of days?

"I suggest you get rid of that thing as soon as possible." With that, she went into the house, forgetting the groceries in her car.

Harley's face burned with embarrassment. She had no idea what to do about her current situation, but she wasn't going to worry about it. She had the Butcher to worry about; she still had time to deal with the other. She couldn't allow her mind to drift too far into the pregnancy because she worried it would drive her into an insane asylum. She was surprised she wasn't already there. How much more could happen to her before she finally snapped?

She got up and walked to Savannah's car. She popped the trunk and started lifting grocery bags out. She got a few in her arms and walked back up to the house. When she opened the door, she heard Savannah talking to someone. She slowly let the door latch silently. Moving stealthily, she set the bags down by the door and moved towards the sound of her voice. She was in the kitchen again, talking on the landline. Her back was to Harley, and she was whispering on the phone.

"This needs to end now; I can't wait any longer. What's taking you so long?"

Harley snatched the phone out of her hand and said, "Who is this?" into the phone.

"Hello, my darling." The sweet drawl of Rayland's voice resonated through the line.

"Fuck." She looked at Savannah, her eyes filled with terror, her mouth trembling. Harley slammed the phone into the receiver.

"Fuck, fuck, fuck." She was slamming the phone repeatedly. She grabbed the base of the phone and ripped it from the wall, throwing it across the kitchen. The phone landed in the sink.

Savannah was shivering beside her, her skin as pale as alabaster, her mouth hanging on the ground. Harley turned on her. "You selfish Bitch. You've been talking to him this whole time. How could you? How could you do any of this?"

Tears were streaming down Savannah's face now. "He told me that he would keep me safe if I lured you here."

"Oh my god. This whole time. You never really needed help. You were just trying to get me here? You sick woman. You have led so many people to their deaths because of your attachment to that monster."

"I didn't mean to. I didn't want anyone to get hurt; I was just so scared."

"Danny is dead," Harley roared at her. "You should have been there at the crime scene to see what you've done." Harley was shaking; all she could see was red. She took a step back from Savannah, afraid of what she might do to the woman.

"Is he here now? Down the street? Where is he?"

"I don't know where he is. He said he took a trip."

Harley stared at her dumbfounded. The woman was clueless, lost, and manipulated by a man she despised.

God, what if he knew that she was pregnant? She couldn't even bring herself to ask Savannah. Would he be happy by the news or angry? She didn't want to find out. She turned and left the kitchen. Savannah was trailing behind her. She walked up the stairs to the second floor and went into the spare room. She started packing her things, throwing whatever she could into the suitcase.

"What are you doing?"

"I'm getting the hell out of here. Do you think, for a minute, I would stay one more night in this trap?"

"No, you have to stay here. I don't know what he'll do if he finds out that you're gone."

"I don't care what he does to you at this point."

"No, you have to stay," she was screeching now, pawing at Harley's suitcase. Harley left it there and moved around Savannah. She needed to get out of the house, away from the clutching hands of Savannah. The woman was a demon and Harley needed time to think. She hurried down the stairs, leaving Savannah in the room. She didn't follow behind her. Harley hurried to her vehicle and slid inside quickly. She locked the doors immediately and assessed her surroundings. Her eyes flickered to each bush, the corners of the houses, the people walking down the sidewalk. Had he been here the whole time. Had he been watching her ever since Danny was murdered? What was he waiting for?

The police officers were no longer monitoring the

outside of the house. The moment that the FBI showed up, they were sent away for whatever good they did. She wished now that they were there. Any added protection would be essential. She put the SUV in reverse and started backing out of the parking spot she had on the street. Maybe it wasn't smart to leave on her own, but she knew she couldn't just sit there with Savannah and not want to kill her for what she did. She refused to be a sitting duck to protect Savannah any longer. She headed to the nearest Starbucks and pulled into the parking lot. She parked, got out of the vehicle, and hurried into the building. She had watched the rearview mirror the entire time and hadn't seen anyone following her there, but she still felt watched.

She ordered a vanilla latte and waited for the drink to be made. She got lost in the sounds of the coffee machines coughing and spitting out the drinks. She pulled out her phone and texted Riley, knowing he would still be in his meeting. There was certainly no need to call off the investigation now; they had all been duped. They would need a new game plan, a strategy to get the upper hand on the scenario before the Butcher killed them all.

She told him to meet her there when he was done and that she would not be returning to Savannah's home.

She sat down on an empty couch, her fingers trembling as she set down her latte. She stared off into space, unsure of what to do next. She thought back to the call that Savannah had made to her while she was still in New York. She had sounded genuinely scared and in need of Harley's help. At what point did the Butcher get in contact with his mother? Had he really been outside her house that day, and if so, did they just make a connection where she agreed to help him? Tears formed in her eyes. She really had dragged Danny into danger. It was never about keeping Savannah safe or luring Harley in. She was the bait from the beginning; she was just supposed to end up dead in the end.

Here, eyes flickered as a couple entered the coffee shop. She expelled the breath she was holding. She had no idea where the Butcher was and whether she was being watched. She smiled finally as she thought about ripping the phone out of the wall. Savannah wouldn't be able to contact Rayland as easily now. She would have to talk to him at some point, and then what? Would the FBI arrest her for her involvement? Possibly, but the entire situation was much more complicated than that.

She couldn't stop looking at the parking lot through the glass windows. She watched any new vehicles coming and going. She had to watch for Rebecca as well. It wouldn't be hard to notice a pretty, young blonde with a pixie cut, so she wasn't worried about her getting past her. The one she was worried the most about was Rayland. After what she saw at Danny's crime scene, she hoped to never see him again. He was the most dangerous and terrifying human that she had come into contact with.

She checked her phone to see if Riley had messaged her back yet. Nothing. She started looking at rentals nearby on Airbnb to see where she could stay for the evening. She didn't want to stay at a hotel because Rayland could stop by each one and look for her, whereas if she got a rental, no one would actually know where she was.

She felt stupid. She had allowed Savannah to contact her again after she had gone to Georgia. She should have stayed there and helped with their case, but she felt responsible for Savannah and wanted to help. Had she stayed in Georgia, the Butcher would have found her either way because he was already there. He had collected Rebecca to go on a killing spree together.

She sipped on her latte as she booked a room for the night. She would decide how much longer she wanted to stay in New Orleans after she talked to Riley. She didn't see a benefit to her fleeing the state, as Rayland would just follow her. But she couldn't possibly continue to work with Savannah and stay with the team. It was just too dangerous.

TWENTY

HARLEY WATCHED AS RILEY CAME into the coffee shop and rushed over to her.

"Holy shit! I got here as soon as I could. I probably broke a dozen laws on my way."

She looked up at him. She wasn't sure if she stopped shaking the entire time.

"Where is Sheldon?"

"He went ahead to Savannah's place. I've never seen him so mad. I wouldn't be surprised if she wasn't taken out there in handcuffs. The hits just keep on coming."

"He must be here somewhere. It wasn't the first time I caught her on the phone whispering to someone. He might have been here all along except when he went to get Keri."

"Yeah, it's hard to say. I'm not sure what he's waiting for though. If he's been here this whole time, why hasn't he struck yet?"

"Well, now he has a new pet."

"Two serial killers in one place. That's not good for us. Especially when we've been staying in the enemy's home."

"What do we do now?"

"Well, we're going to go back to the house."

She shook her head. "I'm not staying there."

"You don't have to. But you should probably grab your things. We need to properly interview Savannah about what she knows, and you should be there. I don't know what we're going to do about her yet. We need to weigh our odds; we might need her."

"She belongs in jail."

"You're right, but we might need her before all of this is done. Let's get the next plan in place, and then if you want to head somewhere else for the night, then it's fine. But if you're going to stay in New Orleans, then you need to be involved in this."

She nodded. "What did the Director say?"

Riley smirked. "He told us to shut things down. We were supposed to pack things up and go back into the office. The Director of the FBI doesn't want to continue paying us to be on vacation in New Orleans."

Harley rolled her eyes.

"Of course, that all changes now that we have had contact again. Especially knowing that Savannah walked us all into a trap. There's no going home now. The trap was to get you, so we can't have you leaving town now."

"I don't plan on it. I want this over with."

"Okay, let's go interview Savannah."

The two left the coffee shop, but Harley was aware of her surroundings the entire time.

TWENTY ONE

HARLEY GAVE SAVANNAH A SCATHING look when she walked back into the house. Gone was the spirited redhead that would put you in your place if she felt like it. She was a shell of her former self. She sat at the kitchen table, shivering as if she was cold, her eyes downcast. When she looked up at Harley, she immediately turned her eyes down again.

Sheldon was standing in the kitchen, his back leaning against the kitchen counter. He was drinking black coffee out of a white porcelain mug.

"Whoa, what happened to the phone?" Riley asked.

Sheldon laughed. "Oh, Harley didn't tell you that she ripped it right off the wall?"

Riley turned to her, a shocked look on his face. "I'm impressed."

"Don't be. That's what happens when you find out someone betrayed you." She said as she stared at Savannah.

"Well, it's a good thing we have cellphones."

"She doesn't." She looked back at Sheldon. "Where are we?" She asked him.

"Well, this has turned into a complete shit show. I didn't expect Savannah to have turned against us. I'm sorry, Harley, really. Your life has been put at risk in unacceptable ways. All of ours have. Savannah didn't care one bit who lived or died."

"That's not true," she croaked. "I was just so scared of him. He's capable of terrible things."

"Yes," Harley said slowly, "No one knows that more than Danny." She looked over at Sheldon.

"Are you arresting her? For obstruction of justice at the very least."

Savannah balked.

"No. Savannah here has agreed to be cooperative now. We'll be keeping an eye out on her."

"You can't trust her."

"Oh, I don't plan on putting any trust in her. But right now, she is a key to the Butcher and I'm going to use it while I can. We have some officers here, and she will be guarded now at all times. If she pulls anything, she'll be going to jail."

Harley sat down at the table across from her. "When did Rayland contact you first?"

Savannah's mouth trembled. "Almost immediately. I played it tough. Told him he better stay away, and he said that he needed my help." She looked right at Harley as she said it. "I laughed at him. Told him I was going to call the police but then he told me to look outside the front window. I did. He was standing there, just staring at me through the window. I don't know where he came from or how long he had been there. He was talking to me on a phone while watching me."

"Where would he have gotten the phone?"

"It's old. Like one of those old burner phones. Rayland is very resourceful."

"Apparently."

"That was when he told me that he needed my help to get you there."

"And you just went along with it as if my life didn't matter," she said bitterly.

"He told me that he would kill me. What else was I supposed to do?"

"Think about someone other than yourself, just for once, Savannah. Think about all the lives you have affected over the years because you just worried about protecting yourself from Rayland."

Savannah glared at her and got up from her chair. "I'm leaving."

"You're not going anywhere," Harley yelled across the table.

Savannah immediately sat back down. "He's going to know that something's wrong, and he's going to come and kill me."

"You're not going anywhere," Harley repeated. "Tell me what happened next."

"He didn't come in the house; he wouldn't cross

that one boundary that I gave him. To stay away. He told me he would kill me if I didn't help him. He told me he would come in right that minute and do it. I told him you wouldn't come. Why did you come?"

Harley was 'this' close to getting up out of her chair and striking her. "You begged me, Savannah. I would have to be pretty heartless to completely ignore you. And if you remember, I did leave once to go to Georgia, and you fucking called me back. Why couldn't you just leave us alone?"

Savannah sulked in her chair. Harley was repulsed by her. Maybe she was always evil, just like her son. She certainly was weak. Unable to stand against a monster, she allowed so many people to die when she could have saved them.

"Did you really not know that there was a body in your backyard?"

"I knew nothing about that, I swear."

"And we should just believe you now?"

"I don't really care what you believe."

"I bet you don't."

"You don't know what it's like to worry for years that he might come back. You've only known him for a few months. I've known him his whole life, and I've feared for my life for 20 years. You have no idea what that's been like."

Harley sighed. She refused to get drawn back into sympathizing for that woman. It would only get her killed.

"Did you tell him I was pregnant?" she whispered.

Savannah shook her head. "He won't be happy."

Harley met her eyes and a chill crawled up her spine. She felt anxiety build up inside of her.

Sheldon spoke up, filling the silence that threatened to suffocate Harley. "He doesn't like children, is that it?"

Savannah turned to look at Sheldon, who appeared as unbothered as ever as he drank his coffee. "Anything that is going to take attention away from Rayland is not good. He obsesses over people. If I would have had another child, something surely would have happened to the child. He will not accept Harley loving that child more than him."

Harley didn't know how she felt about being pregnant, never mind the idea of loving the Butcher's child. She suddenly felt ill. *What the hell was she going to do?*

"He doesn't feel anything. Do you think he would love that baby?" She was practically snarling at Sheldon. "It wouldn't have benefited me in any way to tell him. If anything, he might have just come and killed us all."

"Heartwarming," Riley muttered.

"What was the plan, Savannah? When is he coming here?"

"I don't know."

"You're lying."

"I'm not. I have no idea. That's why I was getting anxious a few days ago because I didn't know where he was or when he was showing up. He wouldn't tell me. He said that he had to clean things up and that when he was done, he would come for you."

"Is he planning on killing me?"

Savannah suddenly looked sad. "I don't know. He changes his mind a lot. One minute, he loves you and wants you to go with him. The next, he's angry and wants to punish you. I don't know what he wants."

Harley felt dizzy and walked out of the room. She walked straight to the bathroom and closed the door behind her. She slowly sat down on the floor in front of the toilet. She vomited generously into the toilet. It seemed endless until there was nothing left. Her throat burned, and she started crying. There was a really good chance that she wasn't going to make it out of there.

There was a knock at the door. She ignored it, but the door opened anyway. Riley stared down at her.

"How's it going in here?"

"We're all going to die," she whispered.

"Well, aren't you just a ray of sunshine now."

She laughed. She wiped her mouth. Climbing off the floor, she went to the sink, turned the tap on and scooped water into her hand. She rinsed her mouth out, spitting it back into the sink.

"Riley, you don't know what we're up against."

He leaned against the door jam. "He's not my first serial killer, Harley. I might not know him exactly, but I'm aware of just how dangerous he is. I've got both eyes open, and I'm not taking any chances."

"I can't stay here. I'll have nightmares. I'll assume she's trying to kill me."

"I don't blame you. But I need to know where you are, Harley. You just can't go into hiding."

She nodded. "I'll send you a link."

They left the bathroom. "Where do you think he's been this whole time? He's been gone for almost a week. Who is he killing now?"

"I don't know. I can't say that I've ever known a killer willing to travel across the country for revenge. It definitely makes it difficult to keep track of him."

"And why Rebecca? What is that? What is his game plan with that?"

"Have you considered the idea that he's trying to make you jealous?"

"I hope you're joking. I mean, I've never considered him completely deluded. He's a psychopath, for sure, a very smart one. But I don't really think that he believes there's a chance I love him. The moment I found out who he was, I tried to ruin him."

"Maybe he found a partner in crime."

She laughed. "Oh god. What a mess. At least that means she's far away from her daughter."

There was a ding on her phone, and she pulled it out of her pocket.

"Oh geez, I should probably check my email more often. My office inbox is full. I need to go grab my laptop."

"Okay, I'll be in the kitchen. I have some more

questions for Savannah."

"Good luck with that." She made her way back upstairs. She went into the bedroom that she was staying in. Her suitcase was still open, her items strewn about. She had to pack anyway so that she could leave for her rental. She carefully folded her clothing and placed it neatly in the suitcase that time. She went around and collected her skincare items and makeup. She did a double check around the room to see if she left anything else before she closed the suitcase. She hoisted it off the bed and set it outside the door.

She went back inside the bedroom to grab her laptop from the nightstand. She needed to go through her emails and make sure there wasn't anything pressing. She had checked in with Roxie a few times while she had been gone, but the poor girl was basically running the office herself. That wasn't fair, but Harley figured since she had a serial killer after her, that she had good enough reason.

But she did have some time while they tried to figure out what to do with Savannah. It would allow her a few minutes to check her emails and get caught up. She immediately got rid of anything that looked like junk. There were a few old emails about a week old that she looked at. It seemed like there were new cases that Roxie wanted her opinion on. They would have to be put on hold for now because she didn't have time to look into them. Maybe tomorrow. Harley had tried to protect Roxie from the gory details about Danny, but she heard the rest of the details from the news, and Harley felt like crap over that. She put her head in her hands, feeling suddenly like a complete failure.

She responded to a couple of emails and then just stared at her inbox. One email, the most recent one, caught her eye. When she read the subject line, her whole body went cold.

Subject: Darling

No, no, no, no, no. The email had an attachment on it. She clicked on the email, and there was nothing in it but an attachment of a video. She knew that whatever was on that video was not going to be good. She wondered if it was a video about Danny's death. She knew for sure that she didn't want to watch that. But she had to know what was on the video. Her hands shook as she clicked on the video, and it started to play. Her screams were heard all throughout the house.

TWENTY TWO

A CUP OF TEA PRESENTED itself in front of her. She looked up and gratefully, yet begrudgingly accepted it from Savannah. She hadn't spoken a word since seeing the video. She took a sip of the tea, a taste of peppermint and lemon electrifying her tastebuds. Harley could finally admit that she was not okay; maybe she hadn't been for a really long time. She was in the living room, and she could not ever erase the things that she saw on the video. Those images would never leave her mind; they would haunt her dreams until she went mad. She was surrounded by men in the room, aside from Savannah, who was looking a little haunted herself.

"I guess we know where he's been all this time. New York. The man has no limits," Sheldon muttered. "Guys, do a perimeter check, be thorough." He barked orders to the officers. Savannah also left the room. It just left Riley and Sheldon in the room with her.

Riley sat down beside her. "Harley. Harley."

She looked up at him.

"I saw the video, and I'm really sorry."

"I haven't seen her in years. The last time that I saw her, I was in a gas station, grabbing milk. I turned around, and she was there, right in front of me. She didn't recognize me, or she acted like she didn't anyway. I couldn't believe how much that day hurt. How much it bothered me that she didn't acknowledge her own daughter in front of her."

Riley was silent. Words really didn't matter.

"Why would he go after her? I literally told him I hadn't seen her. It's not like he thought we had this strong bond. I don't even know her. I grew up thinking my mother didn't love me. And she didn't. She was a terrible woman, a terrible mother, but she didn't deserve that."

"I don't think it really mattered to him how long it's been since you saw her. She's your mother. She'll be your mother no matter what."

"I think he was getting even because I was with his mother. I can't believe how much it hurts."

"Did you really believe that your mother could die, especially in that manner and that you wouldn't feel something strongly about it?"

The thing that she didn't want to voice out loud was that she didn't know what hurt more, the fact that she was murdered so brutally on video but that the entire time, she denounced any love whatsoever for Harley. Sure, she might have been trying to save herself by saying that she never loved Harley or didn't care about her. But the truth was, Harley believed every word that she said about her in that video. Her mother didn't feel a thing for her, which made the fact that she died because of her all the more tragic. But she refused to have that conversation with Riley.

"How did he know where she was?" Harley tried to veer the conversation somewhere else.

"Prison is a wild place. It's like its own community, its own world."

Harley nodded in understanding.

"Although these inmates are locked up, people assume that they have no connection to the outside world. But that couldn't be further from the truth. People get drugs, money, really anything they want inside. Some inmates have arranged murders while sitting in their cells. There are connections on the outside, people making deals, making arrangements to provide themselves with protection."

"Right, it's their own world."

"The inmates rule it. I'm sure Rayland has his own connections on the outside, or he made some new friends on the inside. Either way, he could have put some feelers out had your mother found before he ever left prison. He's had time to stew, to plan this whole thing out."

"He's certainly angry with me. If he's not caught, Riley, I'm never going to be able to have another human connection again because I will worry that he's going to kill everyone I know."

"We're going to get him, Harley."

"I'm not so sure," she whispered, looking into his eyes. "That woman. He allowed her to just have a free-for-all with my mother. This isn't about someone who killed their kids. She's gone full-blown serial killer at this point. How does that happen?"

"I don't know. People will be writing about these two for years to come. I think it's time to start digging into Rebecca's past to see what makes her tick."

"He's going to kill her."

"You think?"

"Well, he doesn't love her. He's not capable of that, so why keep her around? It might be fun and exciting now as they wipe my world off the planet together. But after, when he wants to go into hiding? I don't see him keeping her around."

"I sent the video to the Director. I think at this point he's going to send a whole team out."

"I need to get the hell out of here."

"Do you want me to come with you? I know you don't like it here, Harley, but I think it's safer for you to be here with us than to be on your own."

Tears welled up in her eyes. "I'm just supposed to close my eyes and trust that she's not still trying to get me killed?"

"There are police all around you now, and we're getting another team. He's coming, Harley, whether we like it or not. Do you really want to be alone when he gets here?"

She shuddered. No, she did not.

She pulled her phone out. She placed a call to Sheriff Judd in Georgia. He picked up on the first ring.

"Harley Wolfhart, how are you doing?"

"I've been better. How are things there?"

"We have some good news. The girl finally admitted that her mother was the shooter. We are issuing a warrant out for her arrest."

"That's wonderful, Sheriff."

"Not that we need it at this point now that she has become your problem. But another arrest warrant can only help."

"The more people looking for her, the better. She'll be going down for more than just the murders of her children. She's been more than complacent in the evil deeds of the Butcher."

"Have you heard from him?"

"Yes, it is more ways than one. He took another victim. It seems as if she's taken the role of apprentice with him."

"No shit. What a world that we live in."

"Everything has turned upside down. We anticipate him showing up here any day now. Any day. It appears as if the rest of his work is done now; it's just me he wants now. I think we're at the end of his game."

"Maybe we won't be sending her to jail. He might do the job for us."

She laughed. "I can't even begin to know what he's

going to do with her. It's all too bizarre. I would love nothing more than to know how the two connected up. It's absolutely crazy."

"I couldn't agree more. We have bets going to see what happens to her."

"How is the little girl?"

"She's still in the hospital. She's going to need time to recover. But she's talking now, and that's a big plus. The counselor is working on her, and they've made a lot of progress. She was really scared that her mom was going to come back and finish the job. I think it actually helped that her mom went missing because she didn't have her there whispering in her ear. I think she feels safer now, which is probably why she let the counselor open the piece of paper this time."

"God, that's so intense. Kids are so resilient, but I can't help wondering how all of this is going to affect that poor girl as she grows up. How does a kid even begin to understand why her own mother would do that to her and her siblings? Pure evil."

"Time. She will have the time now to heal. The counselor is really good, and she'll be okay. It won't be perfect, but she's alive."

Harley looked back and thought about what it was like growing up with her addict mom. She definitely wouldn't consider herself a well-rounded person. She had her issues and hangups, things she never really worked through growing up. How much worse would it have been if she realized that her mother tried to kill her? That she would be growing up in a foster home without her mother or her siblings? She cupped her own stomach.

"What's going to happen to the girl?"

"Too soon to tell."

"She's not going to end up in the foster care system, will she? You for sure have a home for her to go to?"

"No. I don't think so. I mean, we are lining up a foster care family, but she won't go to any type of orphanage. We have a couple that's been working with the agency for a while. They will take her in while we figure out the next steps. But she's still doing rehab in the hospital, so we have time. She's safer in the hospital for the time being anyway."

"Where is her father?"

"No idea."

"Do you think that you could send me what you have on her background? One of the agents here mentioned that we should be looking into her just as much as the Butcher. They are a team now, and we don't know if that's a permanent thing. Maybe there is something in her past that we're missing. Something that ties them together that we can use to tear them apart."

"I can get that to you today. If anything pops up, let me know. We're watching your case from here. Hopefully, the arrest warrant helps both of us out."

"Make sure you keep an eye out on that girl."

"There's an officer at her door at all times. She hasn't had any visitors, though, so I'm not really worried."

"Okay, Sheriff. Thank you, and I'll be in touch."

Harley clicked off the call and told Riley they would get some information that day.

"Maybe we can dig up some dirty little secrets about her. Find a way to get in her head. Hopefully, we'll get another call from the Butcher."

"I don't think so. He's got nowhere else to go. I think it will be a surprise attack at this point."

"I'm sorry about the other thing."

She looked over at him, a deep blush covering her face. "Yeah, that other thing."

"I can't even imagine. Do you know what you're going to do?"

"I could be dead tomorrow, so it seems pointless to dwell on it. I'm just going to try to stay sane until this ends and then go from there. But I would be a liar if I said I wasn't worried that I was carrying something demonic inside of me."

There was silence, and then. "I'm a big believer that monsters are made, not born."

"Then how do you explain Rayland? He wasn't abused or neglected. He had an absent father but no real indication that it affected him negatively in any way."

Riley shrugged.

"Even so…. I can't raise the Butcher's baby. I can't."

He nodded. "I don't blame you. I don't blame you for anything. We're living in a madhouse right now, and it's hard to know who we can even trust. You'll get through this, Harley; you're the strongest woman that I've ever met."

She sighed. "Yeah, I'm getting really sick of proving that point."

TWENTY THREE

THE BUTCHER STOOD AT THE end of Cindy's hospital bed, looking down at the girl sleeping peacefully. The security at the hospital had been a joke. They were one hundred percent focused on worrying about Rebecca getting past the nurses. All the Butcher had to do was flip up a fake badge, and he was allowed access. He had sent the security guard away for a break while he "interviewed" the girl.

He stood there listening to the heart rate monitor. She had bandages on her chest and around her arm. He slowly moved to the side of the bed, watching her carefully. He stared down at her at just the moment her eyes fluttered open. She made eye contact with him and gasped.

TWENTY FOUR

I HAD TO KILL THE *babies. I had to. Cindy is still alive, but the Butcher will take care of it. I've done so much for him. It's easy for him. I had to do it. I just had to.*

Rebecca sat in the driver's seat of a Dodge Ram pickup truck. They had acquired the vehicle from the side of the road near the Airbnb that they had stayed in. It had yet to be reported stolen, but they would have to ditch it soon before they headed towards New Orleans. They weren't taking any risks; they had to move around often and not keep a vehicle for more than 24 hours. If it wasn't bad enough that Rayland was on America's Most Wanted list, a warrant had just been put out for her arrest. Normally, she would have started to feel the walls start closing in, but she didn't. She trusted Rayland explicitly, and he was never worried. He believed that he had a destiny. He believed he was untouchable that he could kill anyone that he wanted and continue to roam free in the world. He traveled with fake documents and had a lot of cash. More than she had ever seen. He would acquire documents for her to go to Spain with him when the time came.

She was waiting for Rayland to return from dealing with Cindy. It was important for them that he deal with the child. She had done everything she could at that point. Then, they would truly be free, just the way that it was always supposed to be. People were looking for her, but no one would expect to see Rayland at the hospital. They couldn't see what they were together, what they were becoming. They were all so very stupid. None of them were as smart as she was. She had a plan, something she had been working on for a long time. She belonged with Rayland; she could see that now. She had always known that. She had seen him before on the news when he was first apprehended in Thailand. She couldn't believe her eyes when she saw him in Georgia, pulling up alongside her as she was leaving the police department. He had been the most handsome man that she had ever seen, and now he was there with her. He had accepted what she had done; he had accepted her without judgment. Now, she would follow him anywhere and do anything for him.

Most women would have reeled from what she had done, vomited, turned away, and called the police. But not Rebecca. She wasn't weak like other women; she had to be tough because that's what her father taught her. She wasn't a crybaby, and she did what she had to do to get her soulmate. Now, he was going to do what he needed to do for them to be together. She wished that she could be there to see Cindy's final moments, but she knew that Rayland was right. The risk was too great, and they needed to be careful.

She watched the parking lot and the people going in and out of the building. The police were making mistakes because they weren't expecting her. Her daughter was in the hospital, seemingly with a guard at the door, but the killer could be right outside, and no one would know. That cop had acted so smugly with her in the interview room, but he didn't have a clue what she was capable of, especially now that she was with Rayland. On the highways, they would be watching for her, but she had a different vehicle. They just needed to stay under the radar.

Rebecca couldn't understand why they were going back for Harley. It was too dangerous. She felt his desire to get revenge would put them in a position where they were either caught by the police or worse. They had found each other and murdered together. Why did he need to go back there to deal with her? She implored him to let it go, but he was obsessed with the idea of ending things in some dramatic fashion.

She watched as Rayland walked out of the hospital with a smile on his face. He didn't fear anything.

TWENTY FIVE

HARLEY MADE HERSELF A CUP of tea. The evening wore past 7pm, and she was trying to settle her mind and body in the hopes that she might get a good night's sleep. Riley had talked her into staying at Savannah's house at least another night, and she had begrudgingly agreed. She doubted she would be able to fall asleep, but she was sure going to try.

She found Riley in the living room on his laptop. He was talking to an officer as they were going over the night schedule. They had a much larger team at the house, and he wanted frequent shift changes so that no one got tired or bored, losing their focus when the Butcher arrived. It was important that everyone stay alert, just in case. They knew when he did arrive, they would all be caught unaware. That was just the Butcher's style.

He looked up from his laptop.

"Did you get the files that Sheriff Judd sent over to you?"

"Let me check. Yes, I have a file from him. He mentions here that they don't have a lot because they just started investigating her. But they did get the search warrant, but I think you know the discoveries, and he mentioned to you already that there was a diary. It's enclosed here."

"Yes, I do remember the diary. He said that he believed that she had tried to kill her kids because of some guy. An old boyfriend or current boyfriend who didn't want kids. She was trying to have a fresh start with him."

"That is nuts. There isn't a woman out there that I would end my kids lives for. I sent the email over to you."

"Thanks. I'm going to my room to start reading. Maybe I can get in her head a little."

"Good luck."

She took her tea with her upstairs and set it on the nightstand. She climbed into bed where her laptop was laying on top of the comforter. She slid under the covers, seeking warmth. She placed the laptop onto her lap and opened it up. It turned on immediately. She went to her email to retrieve the message that Riley had forwarded to her. She clicked on the attachment and the file of Rebecca's diary opened up. It was 75 pages long and she started right in the beginning.

She scrolled through the first page, trying to read as quickly as possible. Page after page, the journal was written much in the same way as a love letter. It was like she was talking to the man she loved, not writing a diary entry. Throughout the diary, she pleaded, almost begged this man to come back into her life. She was desperate without him, the loneliest that she had ever felt.

She continued to read, assuming a name would be mentioned at some point, but there never was. Not once, throughout the pages, did she ever put a name to the man that caused such an obsession. And it was an obsession. She was infatuated with that man; there was nothing normal about her love for him. She wanted to possess him and equally have him possess her back. She kept saying in the letters that the children wouldn't bother him, that if he just gave them a chance, he would grow to love them. She would go back and forth, saying she could hire a nanny so that they wouldn't be a bother to him. Page after page, she wrote about her undying love for him, and there was never mention of her children.

No thoughtful stories about being with her children or the things that they got up to. No words of undying love for them or how much she loved being a mother. The only time she mentioned her children in the 75 pages of diary entries was when she was talking to her lover about how much her children wouldn't be in the way.

It was so obvious; Harley wasn't sure how Rebecca could have ever denied what she tried to do. She begged and pleaded in her diary for her lover to come back. He obviously never had, or she would have no reason to continue to beg in the diary. Her children had got in the way of her being with him. Maybe he didn't like kids or never intended to be a father. Either way. At some point, Rebecca had realized that it was her kids that were keeping her from that man. So, she decided to do something about it. She chose the most heinous thing, to remove her children from her life so that she could start over with that man. Was he really that worth it? If he really loved her, wouldn't he want to be part of her family? It certainly wasn't a true love story, not when it came at the expense of her children's lives. What kind of mother could do something like that?

Who was the guy? Had she completely forsaken him when the Butcher picked her up in Georgia? The man was good-looking but was that enough to erase the love she had for that other man.

She picked up the cup of tea and sipped at it as she pondered the diary. She wouldn't mind talking to the ex-boyfriend to find out why he decided to break things off with Rebecca. Whether he ever would have thought she would be capable of murdering her children to be with him. She picked up her phone and made a call to Sheriff Judd. He picked up the call.

"Harley, I'm just leaving the hospital. I was visiting Cindy to see how she was doing."

"How is she?"

"She's much better. I really think she's okay to pull through all this."

"I was wondering if you had a phone number for a family member of Rebecca's. I wanted to see if I could find out a little more about the guy that she's talking about in her diary. Does she have any close friends?"

"I could give you the number for her parents. To be honest, I don't think that she has any close friends and I have no idea who the guy is. She has a typical narcissistic personality, which means that she only thinks about herself. It's hard to make friends like that."

Harley laughed. "Yeah, I pegged her as a narcissist from the beginning. Not to mention an absolute psychopath."

"The parent's names are Robert and Sandy Burch. The phone is 404-292-0090."

"Okay, thank you. I'll let you know what I find out."

She clicked off the call. She opened up her keypad to make another call when her phone rang. She jumped, dropping her phone into the bed. "Shit."

She snatched her phone up and clicked on the call. "Hello there, darling. Miss me?"

She froze.

"Are you there, Harley?" She swallowed hard. Her stomach started turning. "Where are you, Rayland?"

"Ahh, you do miss me."

"Not hardly."

"Be nice. I don't like it when you're mean to me."

Tears started rolling down her cheeks. She didn't even realize it was happening until they started dripping down onto the keyboard of her computer.

"My mother." She choked out. "How could you? And then you sent me that sickening video to watch it. I'll neve—"

"Guess where I am."

"What? What are you talking about?"

"You'll never guess where I am."

She glanced at the bedroom window. Was it finally time? She slowly got up from the bed and made it to the bedroom window. She slowly peeled back the curtain and peeked outside. She could see the cruiser in front of the house, the two officers inside. Thankfully, still alive. She looked down the street, but she couldn't see anything.

"Harley? Are you there?"

"I have no idea where you are." She whispered.

"I'm standing in the hospital room of a beautiful little girl. I'm right at the end of her bed, watching her sleep so peacefully."

She snapped upright. "No."

"Yes, little Cindy. What a sweet child. I'm about to introduce myself and then I'll be seeing you soon."

"No, Rayland. Wait. Rayland, no."

The line went dead.

She threw herself across the room and went through the bedroom door. She was halfway down the stairs when she started screaming for Agent Dawson.

Agent Walters and Dawson came to the bottom of the stairs first just as she got to the bottom. There were two other agents coming into the room that she didn't know.

Savannah hovered at the entrance to the hallway. She wasn't quite sure how to act around Harley.

"What the hell is going on?" Agent Walters barked.

"He's at the hospital."

"What hospital?"

Realization came across Riley's face. "No fucking way."

"You have to go."

"What happened, Harley. Goddammit. Start talking."

She filled them in on the brief phone call she had with Rayland. The fact that he was now currently in Cindy's room.

"There's only one reason for him to be there. Rebecca must have convinced him to finish what she started. That way, there are no further witnesses in her case. He's going to kill her, Riley. My god, maybe he already has."

Agent Walters was on the phone making a call to the Georgia hospital where the little girl currently laid. He was snapping at one of the nurses that answered his call, telling her that she needed to check the girl's room.

"Riley, you have to go. Even if Cindy is fine, he's in Georgia. He won't leave until the job is done. He must be trying to protect his new girlfriend."

"We can't leave you here."

"I'm fine. I'm not allowing Savannah out of my sight at this point. She can't be trusted anymore. He's not here. He's thousands of miles away. I'm not the one in danger right now. Cindy is, and she needs your help. She has two monsters after her."

Riley looked at another agent. Was it Agent Reed? She couldn't keep track of them.

"Get me a private jet now. Let me know where we need to be."

He checked his watch. They weren't that far from the international airport. "We should be able to get there quickly."

Agent Reeds returned. "They're fueling up the jet now. We need to move."

Agent Walters was off the phone. "The girl is fine, for now. I had the nurse check the room, and there's no one there."

"He's there," Harley assured him.

He nodded. "I told them to contact Sheriff Judd and have him start searching the hospital. We'll get there as soon as we can."

Riley turned to her. "I should leave some of the guys with you."

"It's not necessary, Riley. Just leave the guys out front. You're going to need all the help you can get. You're dealing with two serial killers. I'm not sure which one is more dangerous."

The agents were filing out the door. "Riley, let's go," said Sheldon.

He grabbed Harley's hand. "I'll let you know as soon as I know anything. Keep your eyes peeled. He's a ghost, and we don't know where he's going to turn up next."

"Just save her, Riley. Please. She's already been through so much."

"I will."

She watched the agents leave the home, and she could only pray that Cindy was going to be okay. He had his next target. It would only be a matter of time until he struck again. It wouldn't matter how many people were there. Maybe now they would catch him.

She turned and looked at Savannah standing in the hallway. She couldn't read her expression.

TWENTY SIX

PACING AROUND THE LIVING ROOM, Harley felt like her skin was buzzing. She couldn't relax or sit; she just continued to pace. What was the Butcher's plan? He had the opportunity to kill Cindy, but he left the hospital. Why? It didn't make any sense. Was he just trying to torture her, making her aware that it was going to happen and then drag it out? She was just a little girl. She already lived with the realization that her mother had tried to kill her. Why couldn't they just leave her alone? Of course, Harley knew the reason; he was trying to protect his new girlfriend, and the only way to do that was to get rid of the evidence. Not that she had a chance in hell at that point to be able to deny she didn't shoot her kids. The only way they would stay out of jail would be to disappear. If they were apprehended, the two of them would get the death penalty, or at the very least, life in prison.

She stopped pacing when Savannah entered the

room. She looked like a broken woman now, walking around in a slouch. She could barely meet Harley's eyes. Harley hoped that she felt deep shame for the role that she played in the Butcher's current reign of terror.

"There's no point in worrying; that little girl is as good as dead."

Harley stared at her. "What happened to you?"

"You can't escape him. You know that better than anyone. I tried, and he's still here? You should have left him alone in Thailand, where he was far away from me."

Harley sat down on the couch. "Is that what you believe? Are you really that completely deluded? He was always going to come for you, Savannah. It was only a matter of time. He isn't going to allow you to reject him and just live your life. He hates you. What don't you understand about that?"

Savannah just stared at her, shocked.

"You could have stopped this a long time ago, Savannah, and then maybe all of us would have really been safe."

Savannah turned and left the room without another word.

One of the officers from outside came into the living room. "Sorry, ma'am, I don't mean to interrupt. But I just got a call from our Sheriff."

She nodded. "Yes, what is it?"

"He called regarding the remains that were found in the backyard."

"Oh yes. I actually forgot all about that. What were the findings?"

"He said that your suspicions were correct. It was the young girl that dated the Butcher as a teenager." He looked back down at his pad. "Daisy Parks, I believe, yes, Daisy. The Sheriff will be contacting the parents."

"They're still alive?"

"Yes, ma'am. They moved to the next town over shortly after she went missing. I don't think they could stand to be in the area after she was listed as dead."

She sighed. "Well, at least they will finally have some closure."

"He said to tell you that they want to go over the backyard again just to be sure there isn't anything that was missed."

"Like another body?"

"Precisely."

"I'm sure Savannah will be thrilled to hear that."

"Fuck her."

She laughed. "Exactly."

The officer turned and left. She waited until she heard the front door open and close before she settled herself back onto the couch. She was exhausted, and she considered turning in early for the night, but she wanted to see if Riley called her back with any more news.

She quickly ran upstairs to grab her laptop before returning to the main floor.

She sat on the couch, her legs in a crisscross pattern. She set her laptop on her lap and opened it up. She went back to the diary and started to read through the pages. She felt herself becoming absorbed in her words. Rebecca was so obsessed with the man that her feelings were saturating the paper. She wondered why Rebecca never sent these pages to her lover; did he ever know that she felt that way about him? Maybe he did, and he ran like crazy. A lot of men couldn't handle that kind of obsession from a woman; it could become suffocating rather quickly.

She picked up the paper that had Rebecca's parent's phone number on it. She stared at it, and then she picked up her phone. Robert and Sandy Burch. Just another normal family trying to figure how they raised a murderer. She wondered if they were going to just as delusional as some of the others. Desperately holding onto the hope that their child was innocent.

The phone rang, and it rang so long that Harley didn't think that anyone was going to pick it up. Then, a soft-spoken woman said hello, and Harley asked if she was talking to Sandy.

"Yes, who is this?"

"My name is Harley Wolfhart, ma'am. I'm helping the Sheriff's Department on the case involving your granddaughter, Cindy."

There was nothing on the other line, and then there were sounds that appeared to be soft sobs.

"Sandy, are you alright?"

"Yes, I'm sorry. It's just such a horrible thing. What happened to those sweet babies."

"Mrs. Burch, I was wondering if I could ask you a couple of questions about your daughter."

"I would have sworn on the Bible that she was innocent. My own child. I gave her everything, you know. Everything that I could. I would never have believed anyone if they would have said she did anything to those babies."

"I'm so sorry, Mrs. Burch; I can't imagine what you're going through."

"She broke my heart. Those poor children, and we don't even know what's going to happen to Cindy now. Where will she live? They're not going to give custody to the parents of a killer."

Harley needed to get Sandy to focus on her questions. There were things she needed to know.

"Mrs. Burch, I was reading Rebecca's diary entries. Really, they sound more like love letters to someone. She was involved at one point with a man that she was quite taken with. Is this someone that you met at one time?"

"Oh, that man. Yes, to say that Rebecca was taken with him would be an understatement. They've known each other for many years; they were friends first. We were actually surprised that they started dating. There were rumors…."

Sandy stopped, and silence followed.

"Rumors about what, Mrs. Burch? Any information that you can give me would help a great deal."

"Well, some people thought that he was the father of

Rebecca's children."

"What? But she was married. It's believed that her ex-husband is the father of her children."

"The truth is her husband was not faithful to Rebecca, and she lashed out by also not being faithful. He never asked for a DNA test. I think she was taken up with this other man while she was married. Then, of course, after the divorce, they were together all the time. When he broke things off with her, she was devasted. Over the past ten years, he's gone in and out of her life. There were years she didn't hear from him much at all."

"I really appreciate you telling me this. It puts things in perspective. I don't suppose you ever kept any pictures of this boyfriend. It sounds like he's been in her life for a while."

There was a long pause. "Actually, he looked a lot like that man in the video with her. I haven't seen him in years. The man in the video had a beard, and without it, he looks a lot like him."

Harley felt like she had been punched in the stomach. She swayed a little as she stared off into space. Sandy was still rattling on about the man in the video.

"I'm sorry," she choked out. "Sandy, do you mean Rayland?"

"Yes, Rayland was his name."

"Wait, Sandy, are you telling me the man in that video is the man that your daughter wrote those letters about? That can't be."

There was a gasp on the other end of the phone. "That Butcher man's name is Rayland?"

"Oh my god." It all made sense now. Rayland and Rebecca getting together wasn't some weird coincidence because she was in town. They knew each other. He had probably seen her on the news during her interview and decided to look her up again. They had a history together, and she made it clear that he didn't want kids. Those were his kids. Of course, he was going to help her get rid of them.

"No, it can't be. I've known that man most of his life. He is not out killing people. He's handsome and smart. He would never do the things that those people accused him of. That's not the person we know."

Harley thought she was going to throw up. She didn't know what to say. The whole world seemed completely deluded over Rayland, and at one point, even she had fallen for his charismatic personality.

"Mrs. Burch, his own mother, knows he's a killer."

"Oh, that woman abandoned her child when he was a teenager. She's a terrible human being. I can imagine she doesn't have many nice things to say about him."

"Mrs. Burch. If the man in the video is the man, your daughter dated. He is a killer. There is no point in defending him. He was convicted and sent to prison. It's not even the first time that he's been in prison. It sounds like you don't know who the real Rayland is. If I was you, I would be worried about the fact that he has spent time around your grandchildren."

The silence on the other end was deafening. Then, the soft sounds of sobbing started again.

"I don't know what happened to her. What she did is against God but being with that man after what he's done. I couldn't even watch the news when they were talking about his crimes."

"You didn't recognize him on the news?"

"No, I really didn't. He's been out of her life for a long time. She still talks about him like he's this huge part of her life, but he's not around. I know he likes to travel, but I haven't seen him in a very long time. It just didn't click to me that he was the same man."

"I can understand that might be quite a shock for you, and again, I'm sorry. Have you seen Cindy?"

"Yes, a few times, but there are guards, and sometimes it feels like they are even suspicious of us, which hurts. We would not do anything to harm those children. I wish I could say what went wrong with Rebecca, but I don't know."

"Rebecca had another child, a child that died."

"Oh, that was an accident. Just a tragic accident."

"Are you so sure about that now, Mrs. Burch?"

The woman started crying again. "Oh God, no. Please no. Not the baby."

"What was her childhood like? Was she a happy kid?"

"She was quiet. I can't say that she was an overly happy kid, but she wasn't abused. She had an abrasive relationship with her father because he was really strict, and she often rebelled against that. Her forbade her to date and drink, and of course, she tried to break any rule that he gave her. She was very promiscuous as a young woman and would come home drunk when she was still living with us. She's always had a wild side to her, especially when it came to men. She would fall in love quickly and then be devastated when it didn't work out. Her marriage was her longest relationship, but he wasn't very nice to her."

"Was he abusive?"

"I think there were times where he hit her certainly. I don't know what the extent of that was because she never talked about it. No one really did. My daughter has an explosive personality, so I don't think she was ever an innocent party in that marriage. I think they both did things that were wrong. It makes sense that Rayland would be the father of her children and her not care what happens to them because he also doesn't care."

"What was he like with her children when he was around?"

"Very detached. Rayland was a charming man, and he never had problems having women flock to him. It made Rebecca bristle all the time. But it's just his way; his personality made you want to be around him."

"But not with the children."

"Oh, don't get me wrong, he put on a show so to speak but you can always tell the people who aren't into children. He just seemed awkward around them and was never a big fan of holding them. No one was surprised when he told Rebecaa that he didn't want to have children of his own."

"Do you think she ever told him that the kids were his?"

"God, no. She tried so hard over the years to tell him that the kids wouldn't bother him. She even suggested she could get a nanny, which is preposterous for our family. He had no intention of being with anyone that had children. She never would have made him think those kids were his. He would never have come back into her life."

"Wow. I'm learning a great deal about both of them that I think will help. So, thank you for talking to me about it."

"I wish I didn't learn who Rayland really was. It's scary to think that someone like that was a part of our lives. I mean, he could have killed any one of us, couldn't he?

"Yes, he could have. Anyone who meets the Butcher and lives there is very lucky. Take care of yourself, Sandy, and bring lots of love to that child."

"Goodbye, Harley."

She clicked off the call and tried to absorb everything that she had learned. Rayland was a father, but he didn't want to be. Was he capable of killing his own children? She didn't think that he had an ounce of morality in his being, so why wouldn't he? Killing has been so easy for him.

She dialed Riley's number. After the second ring, he picked up. "Harley, is everything okay?"

"Yes. Or I'm not sure. Have you found him?"

"No, we've combed the hospital."

"Maybe he was never here."

"Oh, he was. He was on the video cameras entering the hospital. He was alone. We're not sure where Rebecca was, but there is no video of him leaving the hospital."

"You have to find him. Bring in more agents and surround that hospital. He might be Cindy's father."

"What are you talking about?"

"He's the guy from the diaries, the one she's obsessed with, the one who didn't want to have any children. It's him. They've known each other for a very long time. None of this is a coincidence; Riley and I think he's going to kill her. You can't let him get to her."

"Holy shit. Harley, trust me, we have no intention of letting him get anywhere near her. I just don't understand why he didn't do it when he had the chance."

"He loves playing games. He has all of us beating to his drum. He has the power right now, and he's loving every minute of it. But if he wants to be with Rebecca, then Cindy has to be dealt with."

"I'm worried about you, Harley."

"I'm not the one that you need to be worried about. I really believe that. These two are in some kind of twisted love story, and Cindy is in the middle of it. Rayland will come for me when he's ready, but not until they have dealt with the problem in Georgia."

She could hear someone talking to Riley in the

background.

"Look, Harley, I have to go. But I'll call you back when I know something. Stay safe. I've checked in with the guys out front and told them to keep their eye out. Not to turn their back on Savannah."

"Well, I'm tempted to get a rental again."

"I don't blame you, but I think we need to keep Savannah under watch. Her phone is now tapped, so she's not having secret calls at home any longer. I really believe that we're coming to the end of this, so we all need to be watchful."

"You be safe as well.

TWENTY SEVEN

HARLEY COULDN'T BREATHE. SHE WAS gasping for air, but nothing was coming. She was choking. Her eyes popped open, and he was there. The Butcher was above her, pushing her into the bed. His big, strong hands were around her neck, and she couldn't breathe. She felt herself starting to pass out, and all she wanted was for the nightmare to be over.

"Miss me, Harley?"

Tears streamed down her face as she started to struggle. What she thought was a nightmare was the Butcher in her bedroom for real, trying to kill her. Oh my god, he was really there.

"Please," she squeaked out.

Just when she thought it was over, that the blackness was starting to descend on her, he let go of her throat. She gasped, trying to suck in as much air as possible. He grabbed her by the arms and pulled her up hard into a sitting position. She couldn't fight; she could barely move as she continued to choke. He moved to the end of the bed while she tried to compose herself. She was still catching up on what the hell had happened to her. What was he doing there? She wiped at her eyes and focused on the room, everything now coming into her view. She rubbed her throat as she looked into the ice-blue eyes of Rebecca, who was returning the look with as much hatred as possible. She had dyed her hair red. Oh God, her hair was red. She wondered briefly if Savannah had set her up again. Where was she? Huddled in some corner hiding? Or was she downstairs somewhere, pleased with herself? The Butcher's voice brought her back to reality.

"You didn't think that your death was going to be that quick and easy, did you?"

"Oh my god. What are you doing here? You called me from the hospital. Was that just a lie?"

"Oh no. I was there. I was right where I told you that I was going to be. Looking down at Cindy, sleeping so peacefully." He chuckled.

"Why didn't you kill her? What was the point in going there?"

She was staring at him, trying to keep him talking. Her body shook as her eyes flickered between him and Rebecca. She was at the mercy of two monsters, and she didn't have her gun. She didn't have a way out of the room as Rebecca was standing by the door. She was trapped. There was no getting out of that situation. Were the cops outside dead, or did these two lunatics somehow sneak by them? She could only hope that they would come and check on her at some point. Or maybe Savannah would grow a conscience in the meantime.

The Butcher's gaze softened, which surprised her. "You know me better than that, Harley. I wouldn't kill a child. I'm not a monster."

She looked at Rebecca and saw her head slowly turn towards the Butcher, her mouth hanging open. Something shifted in the air of the room. She just couldn't pinpoint what it was. But she could feel something changing, and the vibe in the room was much different.

"I just wanted you to think that something was going to happen to the girl because I wanted to hurt you."

"Why can't you just let me go? I had every right to put you in prison. What are you even doing here? You have Rebecca; you should be on a plane by now heading to another country."

He stared at her. "I couldn't possibly start my new life knowing that you were here living your life."

"Fuck you, Rayland."

He smiled. "Rebecca begged me to kill you, but I couldn't give up the pleasure."

Harley looked at her. The woman was still glaring at her, but she felt that her hatred went up a level. "Yeah? You found yourself a nice little psychopath to hang around with, didn't you?"

"Rayland," Rebecca said as a warning. He put up a

finger to silence her. She shifted her weight, coming closer to the bed. It was then that Harley saw the butcher knife in her hand. How fitting.

"Now, Harley, be nice."

She ignored him and focused on Rebecca. She was far more unpredictable.

"How long have you known that he kills people?" Harley was intrigued when she saw Rebecca's lip tremble.

"I had no idea until I saw him on the news for the coverage in Thailand. He had been out of my life for many years. Traveling through Thailand, away from me."

"That didn't bother you?" Harley said with a smirk. "If I found out my lover was butchering people, I would think about my life choices. Though I guess you have your own body count stacking up."

Tears were falling down Rebecca's face now as Harley watched the woman's psyche start to crack. "Well, I'll be honest, it was a shock. He had never mentioned anything like that, and he's always been so gentle and sweet with me. I didn't know what to think at first. All these thoughts start to go through your head, like 'What will my parents think?' or 'Maybe if I love him enough, he will stop,' but the truth is you can't help who you love, and I just couldn't stop loving him. He's my everything, and he came back for me."

"Are you fucking serious right now? You fucking whack job."

"Don't call me that." She hissed.

"Harley, stop. I know what you're trying to do," the Butcher said sternly.

"I don't give a fuck what you think. I'm not sure which one of you is crazier. Her or you." She turned her focus back on Rebecca. "So, this was your plan all along, to kill your kids over this psycho? What is wrong with you? What happened to your other daughter? The one who drowned. Did you kill her for Rayland too, you twisted bitch."

"No…. I… that's not what happened."

"It's exactly what happened. Did you tell him your kids are his, was the baby his too?"

Rebecca gasped and the Butcher's head swung towards Rebecca. He was staring at her when he said, "Don't say that."

"It's true. C'mon Rayland, admit it, upon further inspection, they look just like you."

Rebecca's face was filled with fear, but she wasn't denying anything. He looked at her hard before he moved quickly to Harley, going for her throat.

"I'm pregnant," she shouted.

He stopped right before grasping her throat and stared down at her in shock.

"I'm serious. I just found out. It's yours, Rayland, from the island. I haven't been with anyone else."

"What is she saying, Rayland? She does not have your baby. Tell me she doesn't have your baby!" Her voice was becoming shrill.

He ignored Rebecca and sat on the bed beside Harley. Her whole body tensed as he moved closer to her. She wasn't sure if her utterance saved her life or just ensured even more that he was going to kill her. She couldn't read his reaction at all. His hand came to her face, and he cupped her jaw before moving his hand gently across her face. She didn't think that he had ever touched her so gently, and it terrified her more than his anger. She wasn't sure if he was about to snap.

"A redheaded little baby. Possibly a girl. I gave that gift to you."

A blood-curdling scream pierced the room, startling Harley. Rebecca launched herself at the Butcher, stabbing at him with the knife. He roared as she sliced into his arm. Harley bolted up from the seating position and went to the other side of the bed. She slowly lowered her legs to the floor. She watched in terror as he pushed Rebecca away from him, and she stumbled backward onto the floor.

"What are you doing?" He yelled at her. She could hear Rebecca sobbing.

Harley took the opportunity to make a run for the door, and just as she was about to cross the threshold of the bedroom door, Rebecca's foot stuck out and tripped Harley. She was almost through the door when Rebecca's foot launched her through it. She tried to catch herself before she hit the floor, and it caused her to stumble backward. All she felt was air behind her as she went ass backward down the stairs. Her back hit the stairs midway down, and she cried out. She had too much momentum at that point and continued to roll all the way to the bottom. She could barely move at the bottom of the stairs. She had sharp pains everywhere, and the urge to vomit from the pain was strong.

There was a roar from the Butcher that was unlike anything Harley had ever heard before. "You do not touch Harley. Or my kin."

Harley tried to get up and hissed at the pain. Rebecca was screaming. She was in pain. The Butcher was stabbing her over and over again. The shift had happened.

"You told me you didn't want any children. You told me." Rebecca was wailing.

Despite the pain, Harley pulled herself up from the floor. She knew she was running out of time. The Butcher was killing Rebecca, but she knew that he would come for her next. She moved towards the front door, and something caught her eye in the hallway. She leaned against the wall to get a better look. Plus, the break eased the pain slightly. Savannah was laid out in the hallway, her throat slit and her eyes wide, staring at the ceiling. The cycle between mother and son had finally ended. She wondered if, while Savannah was dying, she regretted keeping her silence all those years.

"Oh, Savannah."

Rebecca's voice was cut short, and Harley knew she was out of time. She limped to the front door and swung it open. Not caring if she left it ajar, she headed down the walkway. She was screaming for help, hoping one of the neighbors would come out and help her. She made her way towards the squad car, but she already knew what she would find there. She hobbled up to the driver's side window and didn't need to open the door to see because the window was smashed in. The officer on that side had his head bashed in. His partner's throat had been slit, and she had to assume the two were double-teamed. They hadn't even seen it coming.

"Stupid, stupid. Why didn't you listen?"

One of the neighbor's front porch lights came on, and it gave Harley just a sliver of hope. She wasn't taking any chances, however, and she opened the driver's door. She bent her head and reached into the car, fumbling around for the officer's gun.

"Harley." A shout came from the house.

She glanced up, only to find the Butcher standing in the doorway of his childhood home. He still held the butcher knife, but it was now covered in the blood of his former lover. Her eyes flickered away because if she continued to look at him, she would start to scream and never stop. Where was the gun? Was he sitting on it, for fuck's sake?

"Is everything okay?"

She popped her head up and saw that one of the neighbors had come out of their house. It was a little old lady with grey curly hair set up in curlers for the evening. It was not at all who she hoped would be her savior.

"Run, go call the police, get some help."

Startled, the woman started to back away, and the Butcher started to move towards her. The woman turned and ran towards her house, but she wasn't moving fast enough. Harley pulled herself out of the car and screamed.

"Rayland, don't. Leave her alone."

The Butcher drove the knife deep into the woman's back, so deep that Harley could swear that she could see the woman's spine from there. Terror gripped Harley, threatening to paralyze her on the spot. She dove back inside the car and put her hands on the dead body, looking for a side pocket in the officer's jacket. She pulled out the Glock and checked to make sure the safety was off. She glanced through the windshield to see that the Butcher had finished with his latest victim. The elderly woman didn't move as she lay in the grass. She winced at the sharp pains that emanated through her body with the slightest of movements. She was pretty sure she had internal bleeding somewhere. It was Harley's fault that the woman was dead. She should have dealt with the Butcher on her own. The noise, however, must have alerted someone else in another house because she could hear sirens. That person had wisely chosen to stay inside of the house and saved their life. The sirens were too faint to be of any help to Harley. She would be dead before anyone got to her in time. She was on her own.

The Butcher turned to her. He smiled, and she

cringed at how handsome his face managed to be amongst all the horror. His smile now gave her nightmares and probably always would. She stepped away from the car door, the gun hanging at her side. He was moving slowly towards her, never in a hurry, always taking his time with her.

"You killed Rebecca." Harley knew she would never understand the Butcher or any of his motives for doing anything.

"I couldn't allow her to kill you. Not you."

"Shut up."

She raised the gun.

"You're not going to shoot me, Harley, you know—"

She fired twice, both bullets hitting him blankly in the chest. He stumbled back.

She was done with hearing his monologues.

Despite being hit twice in the chest, he still moved towards her, faster now, relentless in his mission to get her. She fired twice again; this time, the bullets tore open his throat, blood spraying forward. The force of the bullets launched him backward, and his body hit the sidewalk three feet from her. Her hand shook as she lowered the weapon. She slowly moved towards him, remembering every horror movie she had ever seen. Just when you think the killer was dead, he would launch himself up again. Never dying. She stood above him, staring down. She fired one more bullet straight into his forehead.

It was finally fucking over.

TWENTY EIGHT

WHEN SHE OPENED HER EYES, she didn't know where she was. Suddenly, Riley was above her, talking to her, but she couldn't make out what he was saying. She wasn't sure if she was dreaming again, but at least the view was better.

"Can you hear me?"

She blinked, and it all came into focus, and so did the pain. She winced.

Riley looked behind him; she followed his gaze and saw Agent Sheldon Walters. "Can you grab the nurse? Tell her that she's in pain."

Sheldon left the room silently.

"We'll get you some of that good morphine I keep hearing about."

She laughed, but that only caused more pain.

His smile disappeared quickly as he looked down at her. "I can't tell you how sorry I am for not being there."

"It's not your fault. If anything, I'm the one that sent

you away."

"You weren't wrong. He was there; we just can't pinpoint when he left. He had us on a wild goose chase right up until the end. He truly was a ghost; I've never seen a killer like that before."

"I thought I was dead for sure. They both had me surrounded in the room."

"How did you do it?"

"Fed on her insecurities and made her furious, then as a topper I told Rayland he was the father of her children. The system shut down pretty quickly after that. I made a break for it when the two of them were fighting. I still can't believe he killed her."

"You don't believe he actually cared about her?"

"No, I suppose not. I don't think he can feel anything for anyone. God, I feel like I am dead."

"You want me to list the injuries?"

"Please do."

"You have multiple broken ribs; a few are cracked. One of your rib fractures has caused damage to your liver, and you have some internal bleeding, but they seem to have gotten a handle on that. You also had a concussion and a momentous lump on your head. Your whole backside is a massive bruise. The doctor said you were lucky you didn't break your back with that fall."

"Wow, is that all?" She smirked.

His gaze softened. "You also lost the baby, Harley."

She bit her lips as her eyes welled up with tears. Why did she feel so sad? It's not like she wanted to keep a serial killer's baby, but it's not like it was the baby's fault for Rayland's existence. That was like blaming Cindy and her little brother Tommy for having a serial killer as a father. She had never decided what she was going to do about her pregnancy, but she felt a loss either way. She was glad, however, that she didn't have to make that choice.

"Is it weird that I feel relieved?"

"Absolutely not. You've been through significant trauma this year. I don't know how I would have handled that situation myself. I believe God took take of that situation so that you wouldn't have to. Some things just aren't meant to be, and that's not your fault. It was a terrible situation to begin with."

"Thank you."

A nurse whisked into the room with Sheldon behind her. She attached a new bag to Harley's IV, and it wasn't long before she started to feel wonderful.

Sheldon approached the bed. "I'm glad you're okay, Harley. I would have blamed myself if something happened to you."

"It's okay. It's no one's fault. Not even mine. The woman…the neighbor."

"She's gone. She was gone instantly. No one survived the scene but you. I still can't believe he took out his mother, but I guess I shouldn't be surprised. It's a blessing he didn't go after the child."

"He said that he wasn't a monster. He doesn't kill kids."

"Wow, what a great guy," Sheldon said, his voice dripping with sarcasm.

"What's going to happen to Cindy? Can the grandparents take her?"

"No," Riley added. "Firstly, they're too old, but I talked to the prosecutor of this case, and he said after what that kid has been through, we can't rule out that there wasn't some type of abuse going on at that house."

"The father?"

"He has also been deemed unfit. Cindy will go to a foster care family. We have one set up already with a nice family who has been working with traumatized kids for years. There's a really good chance she'll get adopted. But there's no rush; we want to make sure she's mentally well before throwing too much change at her."

"Does she know her mother's dead?"

"She does. The saddest thing about it was that she looked relieved for the first time since she got to the hospital. She cried, but I think it was because she finally felt safe. Like her mother wasn't going to come and get her."

"That is heartbreaking."

"She'll be okay. You did great, Harley. You finally brought that bastard down. Now he can't hurt anybody again. If you ever want a job with the FBI, I can get you in."

She laughed. "I think I've had my fill of serial killers for a while. I think I will stick with missing persons and cold cases for now." Her eyes started to slowly close.

"We'll let you get some rest. I'll check on you in a bit."

She drifted off into a world where the Butcher didn't exist.

THE NEXT CHAPTER

HARLEY WAS BACK IN HER office in New York, scrolling through her emails. She had a lot of backlogs to go through, and she needed to decide what she was going to work on next. She got up from the desk and started to move boxes filled with files. Roxie buzzed into the room with a cup of coffee and set it on her desk.

"What are you doing? Stop it; you're supposed to be recovering. If you need something moved, I will move it. You're going to pull a stitch. You shouldn't even be back to work already. Don't you know how to relax?"

Harley smiled as Roxie continued prattling on about her lack of sense. She knew Roxie was right, but the truth was that if she didn't stay busy, thoughts of the Butcher would come back to haunt her, and she would start to shake. She woke up every single night in a cold sweat, dripping from a nightmare that included a monster in it. He was constantly pursuing her. If she didn't stay busy, she thought that she might go insane.

She was in therapy again with Dr. Kennedy, trying to work through the trauma so that she might be able to be alone with her thoughts once again. The doctor said she was experiencing some form of PTSD, but she believed that it was a hurdle they could overcome together. Harley needed to work; it made her feel like she was righting a lot of wrongs in the world.

"The new hire will be here in about 20 minutes. I will walk him through the system and what you need him to do, so don't even think of getting up from that desk."

The new hire as if those words didn't flood her with guilt. But the killer was dead; there wasn't anyone stalking her, watching her, or waiting to kill her. Her staff should be safe now. Right?

"What's his name?"

"Chase Maroon."

"He sounds like a cowboy."

"Maybe he is," she said with a laugh.

Roxie left the office only to come back a few minutes later. She was holding a file that she set on the desk. Harley sat back down and opened the file.

"You are expected in court on Monday. Though it's a wonder to me why you would add anything more to your plate."

It had been a few weeks since the Butcher had been killed, and the violence and chaos had been put to an end. Once she was discharged from the hospital, she flew to Georgia to visit Cindy. She wanted to make sure the girl was okay. She seemed to be flourishing now that she felt safe. The doctors said that she could leave the hospital in the next couple of days and head to her new foster home. There, she would continue to see a therapist to work through what happened with her mother. The injuries that she sustained left her with a partially paralyzed hand, but her speech had completely returned to normal. Overall, she was very lucky, and she would be okay. Harley had spent two weeks in Georgia at an Airbnb, visiting Cindy and getting to know her. She was a bright and sweet child, and Harley couldn't get over how her mother hadn't seen how fortunate she was to have such beautiful children. Cindy had admitted that she still loved her mother, though she didn't understand what she had done wrong to deserve getting shot. She still felt that it was her fault somehow that she made her mother angry. She still had nightmares every night about the shooting. She often talked about her little brother, who died that fateful night.

To the surprise of everyone involved in the case, Harley had petitioned to adopt Cindy. She felt responsible for the child. They had both been affected greatly by the Butcher, even though Cindy didn't know it. She had never felt better about her decision, but it would probably be another month or so before Cindy would move to New York to be with her. Her father didn't put up a fight, and maybe it was because he always knew that the children weren't his. She would never tell Cindy about her real father; no child should ever have to find that out; she had been through so much already. Once Cindy was cleared physically and emotionally, she would make the trip. They had set up someone for her to continue therapy within the city. Harley also had to be cleared physically and mentally before the move would happen. She should be home recovering, but she had some time before Cindy would show up. She had purchased a new home in Chelsea so that Cindy could have a backyard to play in. She didn't want to raise a child in an apartment. In the end, she had lost Rayland's baby, and maybe that brought things full circle. She wasn't worried about raising a child that was the Butcher's. If anything, she could ensure that the child never knew about him or turned out anything like him.

She was ready to finally start a new chapter in her life, and she and Cindy would take on the world together.

THE END

A NOTE FROM KIMBERLY

Dear Reader,

I hope you enjoyed this book and the characters as much as I enjoyed creating them. I appreciate your support from the bottom of my heart.

Sign up to my mailing list at **WWW.KIMMILOVE.COM** where you can find the most recent news.

If you would like to leave a review for the book and share your thoughts it would be greatly appreciated.

Stay inspired!

Love,
Kimberly

ABOUT THE AUTHOR

KIMBERLY LOVE is the radio host from Crushing 40 and author of *You Taste Like Whiskey and Sunshine*, *Divine Vengeance*, and *The Dismemberer's Handbook*.

Kimberly is a lover of champagne and lives in Florida with her husband and daughter.

Find her online:
WWW.KIMMILOVE.COM

Printed in Great Britain
by Amazon